The Fallen Ring

Cosmic Crisis

Key Dawkins

Also By Key Dawkins

The Fallen Ring Series
The Fallen Ring (Book 1)
The Fallen Ring: A New Nemesis (Book 2)

First published in Great Britain

Book cover designed by Getcovers.

First edition

ISBN: 978-1-7396186-4-3 (Paperback)

ISBN: 978-1-7396186-5-0 (eBook)

Contents

When you learn to harness the power of your fears, it can take you places beyond your wildest dreams.

Jimmy Iovine

Prologue

Eradax, a being built in the crucibles of cosmic creation, soared through the vast oceans of space. Stars flickered and galaxies whirled in the cosmic flurry around him, his journey leading him to the Cosmic Chambers, where the Superlunary Ones, beings of luminous ether light, were holding their supreme council.

Eradax, usually a herald of their will, approached with unusual aggression. The vast doors to the Cosmic Chambers opened and he entered, his enormous wings ablaze with volatile energy. The Superlunary Ones turned towards him, their eyes aglow with cosmic brilliance.

'I have heard of my supposed discharge,' Eradax thundered, his voice echoing through the celestial chamber. 'How dare you make such decisions without my knowledge!'

The Superlunary Ones regarded him with an otherworldly calm, their brilliant forms pulsating in response to his aggression. 'Eradax, you enter the Cosmic Chambers unannounced and with belligerence. Explain yourself.'

Eradax's radiant form flickered with barely restrained fury. 'Explain? I demand an explanation from you! I have served you for many millennia as a herald, and now you're casting me aside, just like that?'

The Superlunary Ones exchanged glances, their luminous gazes highlighting their inscrutable deliberation. 'Your questions, Eradax, about the cosmos, life, death and reality reach far beyond your role as a herald,' one of them stated. 'And a herald has no business probing such depths. You have dared to seek answers beyond the realm of your destined purpose.'

Eradax was stricken by the decision dealt to him. Never had he imagined it would turn out like this. In earlier times, he had been loyal, adhering to the tenets, even when slightly uncertain, and when others did not. He had carried forth the message, spread the word and maintained order on behalf of the Cosmic Authority. He had wished to become a bastion of the beliefs. The way in which he had acted was evidence of that. But now, on hearing this news, a hurricane was brewing within him.

'I served you faithfully. My every action, every endeavour, was undertaken to make you proud. And the moment I ask questions of my own, you're ready to discard me?' Eradax retorted.

The Superlunary Ones maintained their composure. 'The matter has already been debated. Your coming here has only confirmed the decision. You are to be discharged from your role as herald with immediate effect.'

Eradax, seething with anger, bowed his head. When he looked up again, his eyes burned with ire. 'Then I will seek answers directly from the One Above All,' he declared, taking a step towards the gateway that led above the Cosmic Corridor, the path to the Cosmic Entity that presided over all existence.

The Superlunary Ones, their forms glowing with ethereal power, intervened. A force unlike anything Eradax had ever felt before seized him, bringing him to his knees. Jewelled restraints resembling chains materialised, snaking around his arms and legs.

'How dare you defy the decision,' the Superlunary Ones intoned. 'How dare you seek to enter the Cosmic Throne Room.'

Eradax, his muscles straining against the diamond restraints, shouted, 'You cannot imprison my will! You cannot extinguish me like a mere star! You will hear my voice! I want answers!'

The Superlunary Ones exchanged glances but remained resolute. 'For your insolence, Eradax, you shall be banished. Banished to the farthest reaches of the galaxy.'

Eradax scoffed angrily. 'Banishment? I thought you beings were more reasonable than that. You won't end me, but choose to cast me away like cosmic debris instead?'

The Superlunary Ones, their radiant forms glowing with a transcendental aura, smiled serenely. 'Do you have any final words?'

A moment of silence enveloped the Cosmic Chambers. Then, with a glare that could incinerate, Eradax spoke with cold determination: 'I promise you this. I will remember you all and I will grow stronger, more powerful ... and when I do, I will return, and the universe will feel my wrath. I will find a way, and I will wipe out everything. That, I promise.'

Merging their cosmic powers, the Superlunary Ones sealed Eradax behind a shimmering barrier, the diamond chains morphing into an intricate prison cell that was immediately propelled through the doors of the Cosmic Chamber and sent hurtling through space and far across the galaxy.

As Eradax disappeared into the cosmic expanse, his voice echoed throughout the chambers: 'I will tear the universe asunder. I will annihilate everything. I promise! I will find a way. I ... will ... find ... a ... way!'

Appearing slightly unnerved, the Superlunary Ones watched as Eradax vanished into the cosmic abyss. But the decision had been made, and the consequences would ripple across the fabric of the universe. Tales of Eradax's rage would echo forever.

Chapter 1

The sun beamed over the grand courtyard of City, University of London and excited chatter filled the air. The momentous occasion had arrived – graduation day. Friends and family had gathered to celebrate the achievements of their loved ones, marking the culmination of years of dedication and hard work. Amid the sea of caps and gowns, one figure stood out: Simon Jones.

Clad in his graduation attire, Simon sat among his fellow graduands, his heart fluttering with a mixture of excitement and anticipation. The breeze rustled the fabric of his gown as he gazed ahead at the stage, where university officials and guest speakers were sharing words of wisdom. The realisation that he had successfully completed his studies in cybersecurity and was now about to receive his bachelor's degree was both thrilling and nerve-wracking.

Beside him sat Layla Thompson, the girl he had met at the university and who was now his girlfriend. Her eyes sparkled with enthusiasm as she leaned playfully against his shoulder. Her presence offered him a sense of calm within the throng of students and amid the grandeur of the occasion. His lips curved into a soft smile as he pulled her close.

The speeches continued, a blend of inspiration and encouragement that echoed within the courtyard. Simon absorbed every word, his thoughts drifting between the words spoken and the journey that had led him to this moment: his late-night study sessions, the camaraderie of his classmates and the countless hours dedicated to mastering the intricacies of cybersecurity.

Then the time finally arrived for the graduands to be called up individually. Simon's heart raced as his name came through the speakers, prompting a sense of accomplishment to swell within him. With steady steps, he made his way onto the stage, his stride reflecting the resilience that had carried him through his academic journey.

The moment he received his degree certificate etched itself into his memory. The applause of his fellow students and the cheering from the audience swamped him in a wave of celebration. He looked out into the blur of faces, his eyes locking onto the familiar ones that held unwavering support for him: his mother, Sarah, and his younger sister, Tessa. Their smiles radiated pride, filling Simon with a sense of gratitude. Above the applause, Layla's cheers resonated in the air. Her clapping hands and beaming smile mirrored his own joy and for a moment their eyes locked, reaffirming their shared connection.

As the ceremony drew to a close, Simon and his fellow graduates left their seats to rejoin their families and the courtyard buzzed with a vibrant energy and shared laughter. Filled with anticipation, Simon scanned the crowd for his mother and sister. Finally spotting them, he rushed over, a grin spreading across his face.

'Mum! Tessa!' he exclaimed, his voice laced with excitement.

Sarah's arms enveloped him, her pride evident in the way she held him close, while Tessa clung to him, her enthusiasm matched only by her affection for her older brother.

Within the embrace, Simon's voice softened, a note of nostalgia tingeing his words. 'Wish Dad could've been here,' he said, his tone full of melancholy.

Sarah gently pulled back and looked at her son, a shared understanding passing between them. 'He would've been so proud of you. Both your father and James,' she replied, her voice soft and reassuring.

For Simon, they were the two people with whom he wished he could have shared this euphoric moment of his life.

His pensive moment was interrupted by Layla's arrival, her smile radiant as she approached them. 'Congratulations, Simon!' she exclaimed, her voice a joyful melody.

Simon smiled at the sight of his girlfriend and pulled her in for a side hug. 'You and I both.'

'Mrs Jones, Tessa, it's a pleasure to see you both again,' Layla said, turning to hug them.

'Likewise, Layla. It's always wonderful to have you around,' Sarah said, gently squeezing Layla's hand.

Layla's laughter tinkled through the air. 'Thank you. You've been more than welcoming, and I really appreciate it.'

Sarah gestured towards her son, her eyes twinkling. 'Well, he did say you were the reason he survived his programming classes.'

Layla's eyes danced with amusement. 'I'll take that as a compliment.'

Sarah's expression softened as she regarded the two young adults before her. 'Let's continue the celebrations this evening at a restaurant. You're both invited.'

Simon's face lit up at the prospect of continuing the celebration. 'Absolutely, Mum! We'll be there.'

Sarah exchanged a knowing smile with Simon and gave him a playful nudge. 'You go on, have fun. We'll catch up with you later.'

Simon blushed as he glanced at Layla and then his mum and sister. 'All right, Mum. See you there.'

With a final wave, Simon and Layla headed off, their laughter mingling with the joyous ambiance of the day. With the graduation ceremony now in the rearview, a new chapter of their lives would begin, one that Simon was eager to explore.

CHAPTER 2

The automatic chime of the convenience store door announced Simon's arrival, its cheerful jingle ringing throughout the shop. Inside the brightly lit store, the scent of packaged snacks and fresh newspapers greeted him. Running his hand over his short hair, he patted the raindrops from his head as he moved past the aisles of neatly stacked merchandise. He made his way over to the beverage fridge and eyed the soft drinks, looking for the flavour he desired. Settling on orange, he scooped it up, then considered which one he should get for Layla.

As he reached back into the fridge, the door chime announced another customer. Turning to look over his shoulder, Simon was struck by the strange appearance of the man who had just walked into the store. He wore a black balaclava, and one of his hands was concealed inside his long blue jacket. Following behind him was another man, who was wearing a red balaclava, his hand deep within one of his pockets. With his back to the door, the second man brandished a large knife, holding it low, just below his waist.

Alarm bells went off in Simon's head and the atmosphere suddenly became charged. Something bad was about to go down. Instinctively, he touched his silver Ring, but before he could make a move, he felt cold metal press against the nape of his neck.

'Don't you move,' commanded a feminine but menacing voice.

Simon quickly surmised the situation. A robbery was about to take place, and he was being held hostage. Even for a city like London, armed crime like this was excessive. Whether or not the thieves had murderous intent, he didn't know, but he wasn't keen on waiting to find out. He glanced over to the front of the store where the shop assistant was standing terrified behind the till. The man in the black balaclava pointed his pistol at the middle-aged man and threw a bag onto the counter.

'Fill up the damn bag, bitch, and fast!' barked the thief, gesturing to the bag.

The assistant, with shaking hands, complied with the thief's demands, grasping at the money in the till and stuffing it into the bag.

'Try anything and I'll have my man cut you,' warned the thief in the black balaclava, glancing at his accomplice near the door. The man in the red balaclava raised his knife aggressively as if to demonstrate he would make good on the threat.

The situation was escalating quickly. Simon knew he had to act now. He hadn't intended to use his powers this early, but duty called. His mind shifted gear as he analysed the situation: three thugs, two with guns and one with a large knife. Making subtle movements with his head, he glanced up at the corners of the room and the ceiling. He appeared to be in a blind spot. Perfect. He could stop the crime while maintaining his anonymity.

'Move again and I will shoot,' said the voice behind him, pressing the cold metal harder against his neck.

Hearing this, Simon prepped himself for the decision he was about to make.

You ready? The voice of the Fallen Ring echoed in his head.

Simon took a deep breath. *Yeah. But we don't transform. On my count: three, two, one ...*

As soon as he reached one, Simon spun around and clotheslined the woman who was holding the gun to his head, knocking her unconscious before she hit the floor. Before turning back towards the others, he pulled his grey hood low over his face to protect his anonymity. As he turned to face the front of the store, the man in the black balaclava shouted to his lackey by the door who looked up and launched himself down the aisle towards Simon, his knife clutched in his hand. Closing the distance, the thug lunged at Simon, aiming for his stomach, but Simon was much faster than he had anticipated. Dodging the blade, Simon kicked the man's shin, bringing him down to one knee, before hammering his fist into his face, sending the thug crashing headfirst onto the shop floor.

With two down and one to go, Simon turned his attention to the man in the black balaclava, who ran towards him, his pistol aimed at Simon's chest. But just as he pulled the trigger, Simon's armoured hand shot out and covered the muzzle, quieting the sound of the gunshot and containing the impact. The thief stopped in his tracks, his eyes widening as he looked at Simon's hand in disbelief. Seizing the moment, Simon rammed his fist into the man's stomach, before lifting him up and hurling him into the shelves, rendering the thug motionless.

With the situation diffused, Simon vitiated the criminals' guns by stomping on their barrels and then ran out of the store, past the shop assistant whose mouth was hanging open. He had no desire to draw unnecessary attention to himself, nor could he risk revealing his identity. If his cover was blown, he was certain there would be enough criminals looking for revenge, which was a dangerous can of worms.

The soft drinks would have to wait for the time being.

CHAPTER 3

The city's heartbeat pulsed beneath the velvety blanket of the night sky. A million lights shimmered across the sprawling canvas of London, casting an ethereal glow that painted the urban landscape with a sense of wonder. Above the towering structures and bustling streets, Simon was sitting on a rooftop ledge, his legs dangling over the precipice, looking down on the panorama that lay before him. He found solace in this lofty vantage point. The city's nocturnal symphony, a blend of distant sirens and muffled conversations, served as a backdrop to his thoughts. The wind whispered secrets in his ears, its gentle caress a reminder of the freedom that came with the darkened skies.

His eyes traced the contours of the London skyline, and his mind drifted back to earlier in the day – his graduation ceremony, which had marked the end of one chapter and the beginning of another. The memory of Layla's radiant smile and the applause of his loved ones reverberated in his thoughts. He was older now, a young man whose future was brimming with possibilities. He would soon be starting his new role at a prominent cybersecurity firm. His dedication had paid off, securing him a full-time position after acing the interview. But this was more than a job, it was the first steppingstone in his career, and he would soon leave behind the part-time administrative position that had sustained him during his university years.

He looked down at his hand where the silver Ring gleamed. A gift from the universe, it had granted him abilities that transcended the realm of ordinary existence. A whisper echoed in his mind – the voice of the Ring: *You are no longer the teenager who stumbled upon us*. The resonance of the voice was both enigmatic and comforting. *You have become the bearer of our shared legacy and the Guardian of its potential.*

He traced the outline of the Ring as he contemplated the truth of its words. The journey that had led him to this rooftop, to this crossroads of identity, was a testament to his evolution. The Ring had unlocked doors to power and responsibility, and he had embraced it as best as he could.

Using the Ring's power, he donned his dark-purple alter ego, becoming the silent protector of London's night-time. The transformation was more than physical; it was a shift in identity, an acknowledgement of the dual nature that defined his existence. His alter ego was more than a disguise; it was a reflection of the latent strength within him.

A thrill coursed through his veins as he rose to his feet, his body moving with a grace that belied his other identity. The winds that danced around him seemed to respond to his newfound confidence, as if acknowledging the synergy between his alter ego and the pulse of the city.

With each leap and bound, he revelled in the exhilaration of the night. He scaled walls, leaped across rooftops and defied gravity with a fluidity that was second nature to him now. The city was his playground, a canvas upon which he could etch his signature. The thrill of movement, the rush of wind against his face – it was an expression of freedom experienced by only a select few. Yet despite the rush, his thoughts remained tethered to the responsibilities that accompanied his alter ego. The Fallen Ring had granted him extraordinary abilities, but its power was not to be taken lightly. It was a force that could shape destinies and alter realities, and a temptation that could easily sway even the noblest of hearts.

The voice of the Ring echoed once more in his mind, its presence a constant reminder of the choices he must make: *You've demonstrated that your path is not one of power alone. Balance must be your watchword, for it is easy to tip either way.*

Simon perched on the edge of a rooftop, his eyes closed for a brief moment, his thoughts aligned with the weight of his calling. He wasn't just a young man with ambition; he was a Guardian, a protector, a beacon of hope in a world shadowed by deadly sins.

An intangible tingling vibrating through the air drew him from his thoughts. The Ring's voice grew clearer, its tone alert: *It's time to return to work, Simon.*

Opening his eyes, Simon's resolve solidified. His alter ego was more than a guise; it was an embodiment of purpose. He leaped from the rooftop, his body descending gracefully through the night, a shadow in pursuit of justice. The robbery attempt at the convenience store had been merely the beginning of the crimes he would need to stop tonight.

Chapter 4

The night hung heavy over the city, cloaking its alleys and hidden corners in a shroud of darkness. Among those who thrived in the shadows was a criminal gang of four men. Travelling through the city streets in a black Jeep, they were focused on their next job. In the passenger seat was Daniel Kato, the skilled technician of the group. In the rear seats sat Bennie Blum, the rookie of the group, next to Guner Guzmán, the brawn of the group. In the driver's seat was Keith Barracks, the brains of the group and the man who called the shots. Tonight, he was leading his team to an orphanage for a robbery. The word on the street was that the underfunded charity had recently come into a massive cash windfall thanks to an anonymous donation – over half a million pounds, or so the whispers went. For Keith's crew of career criminals, it was the perfect opportunity – too enticing to pass up.

The Jeep slowed to a crawl as Keith surveyed the area around the old orphanage building. Tucked away on a quiet side street, it seemed deserted for the night. Killing the headlights he coasted to a stop in a back alley around the corner.

'All right, listen up,' he growled, turning to face his men. 'Danny, Guz, you're with me. Benny, you're on lookout duty in the car.'

Bennie's eyes widened in the rearview mirror. 'What? Why do I have to stay behind?'

Keith fixed the younger man with a withering look. 'In case the Guardian shows up. We can't risk dead weight slowing us down if he gets involved.'

A nervous chuckle escaped Bennie's lips. 'The Guardian? That's just a myth, Boss. I didn't think—'

'I've seen him', Keith said flatly, his tone dead serious, 'with my own eyes. He ain't no joke. And if he gets wind of this job, I'm damn near certain he'll try to stop us. So, you're staying in the car and keeping watch. Understand?'

Bennie opened his mouth as if to protest further, but simply gave a small nod.

Keith turned his attention to the others. 'Mask up, grab the kit and duffel bags. We get in, get the money, get out. No mistakes. No distractions. This is a straightforward smash-and-grab, nothing more.'

They pulled on black ski masks, further obscuring their features in the darkness, and placed tools and supplies in a small black bag: Daniel's lock picks and small, shaped charges to blow the safe's hinges if needed. Guner, however, didn't need any tools. He strapped on an exoskeleton suit – a matte-black armoured frame that encased his arms and upper body. Servomotors whirred as the mechanical muscles activated, augmenting Guner's already impressive strength.

Moving quickly and quietly, the three men made their way through the inky shadows towards the rear entrance of the orphanage. The thick metal door looked imposing, but it posed little difficulty for Guner in his exoskeleton suit. Grunting with effort, he heaved against the door's handle with one armoured hand, his other pushing against the frame. Hydraulics hissed as the suit's servo-powered arms engaged. Slowly, but inexorably, the heavy door began to bend outwards, its frame warping and bolts popping loose from the brickwork. With one final heave, Guner ripped it open, the shriek of tortured metal filling the still night air.

The trio slipped inside, their senses on high alert, and wound through a maze of dimly lit hallways, Daniel leading the way with Keith and Guner close behind. The orphanage seemed deserted, not a sound save for their muffled footfall. Eventually, they came upon the small records office where the safe was kept.

Daniel made quick work of the outer door, his nimble fingers working the tumblers until the lock clicked open. Behind the door was a heavy cast-iron safe, its surface smooth and featureless. From the black bag, he pulled out a stethoscope and small drill bit. Pressing the scope against the frame of the safe, he began to drill into the casing to locate the lock mechanism.

While he worked, Keith and Guner kept watch, their eyes roving constantly for any sign of movement. Guner's exoskeleton whined softly as servos autonomically adjusted to keep him balanced and ready to spring into action.

Several tense minutes ticked by before they heard a muffled clunk from within the safe.

Daniel grinned beneath his mask. 'Got it,' he murmured, carefully turning the final tumbler.

The heavy door of the safe swung open with a groan to reveal their hard-won prize: stacks upon stacks of neatly bundled banknotes. Guner let out a low whistle as he pulled the duffel bags off his shoulder. He wasted no time shovelling the cash inside, wads of bills disappearing by the fistful.

As Guner worked, Daniel turned to Keith. 'Tell me again, Boss, you ever think about what we're doing here? Hitting an orphanage for cash—'

'No!' said Keith, his eyes cold and unfeeling. He shook his head curtly. 'No. We do what we have to do. Take what we can, when we can, however we can. Having second thoughts? That's weakness. And weakness breeds fear. Fear gets in the way of opportunity. That's why we don't tolerate weakness, not in this life. At the end of the day, it's a job and this is our payment.'

Daniel was silent for a moment, watching as Guner transferred the remaining money. 'Yeah ... I guess you're right.' He sighed. 'Opportunities like this don't come along too often.'

Grabbing and bagging the last wodge of cash, Guner froze as an alarm tore through the silence of the room. He looked up, panic filling his eyes.

'Must have been a failsafe tied to the safe's weight,' said Keith, his voice a low growl. 'Grab the bags. We need to move. Now!'

They scarpered back through the corridors towards the exit, the high-pitched alarm ringing in their ears and the duffel bags weighing them down.

Outside, the engine of the Jeep roared into life, headlights blazing as the rookie waited anxiously behind the wheel. Keith's heart pounded in his chest as he flung open the boot and they began tossing in the heavy bags of cash. A sense of impending danger was thick in the air, the tension reaching its zenith when Keith eyed something materialising from the shadows. Like a spectre it emerged, forming a humanoid shape.

'Stealing from an orphanage ... now that's an all-time low, fellas,' said the looming figure, its words laced with a chilling certainty.

Keith's breath caught in his throat as cold realisation washed over him. The Guardian, the mythical being that safeguarded the city. He was standing before them, fixing them with his bright-purple eyes.

'N-not you ... n-not now ...' Keith stammered, unable to tear his eyes away.

Daniel recovered first, whipping out his snub-nosed revolver and firing a flurry of rounds as the figure approached. But the bullets were merely absorbed and discarded by the Guardian as he continued to advance undeterred. With a savage grunt, Guner charged the vigilante head on, his exoskeleton suit augmenting his forward momentum into a battering ram of fury. But before Guner could make contact, the Guardian front flipped over him, then turned one of its hands into a tendril-like appendage and smacked the gun out of Daniel's hand. Daniel recoiled and the purple vigilante rushed forward and slammed him into a brick wall.

Keith, rooted to the spot, watched the events unfold as if his mind was struggling to process the supernatural scene playing out before him. But as Daniel slumped unconscious to the ground and Guner attempted to hold off the humanoid, his survival instincts finally kicked in. Spinning on his heel, he sprinted for the Jeep, throwing himself into the passenger seat.

'Get us out of here, now!' he screamed at Bennie, who seemed paralysed behind the wheel, his eyes wide with terror.

Bennie's hands shook violently on the gearshift, his feet working the pedals in a frenzy, desperately trying to find the biting point of the clutch. After several white-knuckled seconds, the transmission finally engaged with a grinding of gears, and the Jeep shot forward, its tyres screeching against the asphalt, putting distance between them and the crime scene.

Keith turned in his seat and glanced out the window. Guner swung a haymaker with his exoskeleton only for the Guardian to catch his arm and twist it before kicking him to the midsection, sending him off his feet and into the wall. Sparks flew from Guner's exoskeleton and he collapsed to the ground in a heap.

In the rearview mirror, Keith caught one final glimpse of the Guardian. His incandescent purple eyes burning in the night, following their frantic escape, unblinking and unflinching. A chill shot down his spine as their eyes locked through the warped glass, the vigilante's glare a promise of pursuit.

The Guardian wasn't about to let them go unpunished.

CHAPTER 5

Adrenaline pulsed through Simon's body as he stood among the shadows, his alter ego exuding an air of vowed vengeance, his eyes narrowing on the tail lights of the black Jeep. He had subdued and tied up two of the robbers with some loose metal chains, but there was no time for respite. Two criminals were fleeing, their attempt at escape further fuelling his resolve to bring them to justice.

With a bound, he leaped onto the ledge of a nearby building, his body merging seamlessly with the night as he took off in pursuit. The world around him transformed into a blur of motion – a symphony of streetlights, billboards and buildings that whizzed by in a breathtaking display of agility. His heart raced as he bounded from rooftop to rooftop, the thrill of the chase coursing through his veins. He was a force of nature, a phantom that hunted criminals.

Ahead of him, the Jeep darted through the streets, carving a desperate and dangerous path between the lanes. But Simon matched its speed, his agile movements allowing him to keep pace as the car weaved through the alleys and avenues of London. These criminals appeared to be a cut above the common ones, but he was confident he could catch them. The Jeep raced on, but his mind remained one step ahead, calculating its course, anticipating the next move. With a final burst of speed, he soared from a rooftop, his body tracing an arc through the air before he landed gracefully on the roof of a nearby building. The Jeep hurtled around a corner, its tyres screeching against the pavement as it barrelled down a narrow street. Simon's lips curled into a determined grin. He knew their course, and there would be no escape.

The night air whipped against his form as he took off once more, his feet barely skimming the rooftops as he propelled himself forward. The glow of the streetlamps cast long shadows that seemed to dance in rhythm with his movements. His breathing was steady and his focus unbroken as he maintained the chase.

Suddenly, his acute senses caught a glimpse of a couple stepping onto a pedestrian crossing, unaware of the impending danger. The Jeep was hurtling towards them, its speed leaving them vulnerable to a collision that would prove catastrophic. Changing course, he surged towards the crossing, his muscles propelling him towards the vulnerable couple. Reaching them in an instant, he wrapped his arms around them and swept them out of harm's way. The screeching tyres and thunderous roar of the Jeep's engine were silenced by Simon's intervention, the world reduced to a tableau of suspended time.

The couple, their hearts racing, looked up at the figure who had saved them. Simon's dark silhouette was a paradox – equal parts guardian and enigma. They exchanged a bewildered look, their eyes a mixture of shock and gratitude.

'You're safe now,' Simon said, his voice a reassuring whisper. And then, as abruptly as he had intervened, he set them back on the pavement, his focus shifting back to the unfinished pursuit of the Jeep that continued its reckless flight, weaving its path through blurred streets and sharp turns.

Simon was relentless now, his pursuit fuelled by the need to put an end to the criminals' desperate escape. They had already endangered a few lives; he wouldn't let them endanger any more. The distance between Simon and the fleeing Jeep began to close as the black vehicle weaved through the arteries of the city, its headlights piercing the darkness in twin beams of defiance. Simon's breath quickened; he was getting closer, his prey almost within reach.

With one final burst of speed, he leaped from the ledge of a building, barrelling through the air in a calculated trajectory and landing on the roof of the Jeep, the impact barely causing a ripple in his fluid motions. From his vantage point, he bent down and peered through the windscreen, his eyes blazing with a mix of anger and excitement. Inside the vehicle, the criminals were wide-eyed with fear, their eyes locked on the fearsome figure that had materialised before them once again. Bennie's hands trembled on the wheel and, for a moment, he lost control as the Jeep veered dangerously close to the edge of disaster, the wheels grazing the high kerb, the sudden impact jolting the vehicle. The criminals' hearts raced, their instincts screaming as Bennie struggled to regain control. But it was too late. The car flipped over, the world spinning in a chaotic whirlwind.

Simon's instincts kicked in as the Jeep rolled, his body moving with a grace that defied the laws of physics. He lunged forward, his arms extending to catch the vehicle just above the pavement, the sheer strength of his alter ego bearing the considerable weight. Holding the car aloft, he planted his feet, his muscles taut as he stabilised the vehicle above him. With a powerful thrust, he righted the car in a fluid and controlled motion. The Jeep landed on its four wheels with a muted thud, its momentum completely halted.

Inside the car, Keith and Bennie slumped in dazed silence, their senses reeling from the violent upheaval. In the passenger seat, Keith cowered before the Guardian's intimidating form.

There was nowhere to run now.

The impasse was shattered by the sound of approaching police sirens, their wailing chorus drawing nearer with each passing moment. Simon glanced towards the flashing blue lights in the distance. It was time to leave. Reaching inside the vehicle, he restrained the criminals within their seats, his actions precise and efficient. He met their panicked gazes with a stern threat: these were his streets to protect. His city.

As the sirens grew louder, the Guardian cast a final glance at the criminals, his eyes vigilant and judging, before he merged with the shadows, his figure fading into the obscurity of the night once more. It had been another successful night of stopping crime. The pursuit had ended, but it was only a taste of what was to come.

Chapter 6

In the scorching embrace of the Egyptian desert, beneath the unrelenting sun, a small group of Bedouins went about their daily rituals. Their tattered garments billowed in the hot breeze as they shepherded their herds of camels and goats across the shifting sands of the endless dunes, a harsh terrain seemingly untouched by the passage of time, where nature reigned supreme.

Amid the bustle, a solitary figure glanced upwards, his eyes drawn to the azure-blue sky. A blazing light, akin to a falling star, streaked across the sky, descending with an uncanny swiftness that defied explanation. With a thunderous impact, it collided with the desert floor, sending forth a billowing plume of sand and dust.

Awestruck and bewildered, the Bedouins drew closer to the impact site, their curiosity mingling with trepidation. Before them lay a strange pod, its surface shimmering with an otherworldly luminescence. They exchanged wary glances and spoke in low voices hushed by fear and anticipation. What was the meaning of this foreign object?

With a unified gasp, the shepherds took a step back as the pod underwent a metamorphosis, a transformation that defied the boundaries of earthly comprehension, and a figure emerged. Towering above the Bedouins at an imposing nine feet, the being exuded an aura of alien majesty. Its body bore a carapace-like armour, a mosaic of intricately designed plates forged from a celestial metal. Fiery yellow eyes pierced the air with an intensity that sent shivers through the onlookers.

'I ... am Eradax,' the being declared, its voice resonating with an eerie cadence. It was a name that resonated with cosmic significance, and in that moment the Bedouins cowered in the presence of a being that surpassed the limits of their most vivid imaginations.

Fixing them with a deathly glare, Eradax watched as the desert dwellers turned on their heels, fleeing for their lives. And so they should. If the humans truly valued their lives, there was no other choice but to flee. To stay, would be to die.

With the dwellers dispersed, Eradax stood alone, a solitary sentinel among the yellowly dunes. His eyes, devoid of emotion, turned towards the distant horizon where the ancient pyramids rose like monolithic giants. To Eradax, the structures themselves were of little significance, their architectural grandeur archaic remnants of civilisations that had long since withered. However, the great pyramids beckoned him; they were a key part of his mission. With deliberate purpose, he set forth across the desert, his colossal strides spanning the dunes effortlessly. Many millennia may have passed since he had last ascended the stars, but his resolve remained unchanged.

The pyramids loomed, and as Eradax neared the ancient monuments, he scrutinised their stone facades. But they were nothing more than symbolic markers of a bygone era. His interest was drawn to something else, something concealed within the pyramids' shadows – the object of his pursuit. Somewhere within these ancient structures lay a device, a relic that transcended the boundaries of time and space: the Infinity Forge, an indestructible device that held the power to extinguish all life across the cosmos, to erase existence down to the very last atom. Eradax's intent was unequivocal: to grasp the device and claim dominion over the universe itself.

But Eradax's insatiable hunger for annihilation revealed another truth – an ultimate truth that would shape the fate of the world. To harness the device's apocalyptic capabilities, he needed not only the Forge but also a Fallen Ring, to create a fusion of immense power. Eradax's path was not just one of conquest; it was a collision course with destiny.

Eradax advanced towards the stone pyramids, each footfall an extension of his indomitable will. The shifting sands of Egypt bore witness to his inexorable march towards a destiny set for cosmic eradication. As he closed the distance between himself and the pyramids, the fabric of reality trembled, for the arrival of Eradax marked the advent of a cataclysmic era – an era where the universe itself hung in the balance.

Chapter 7

The early morning sun cast a golden hue over the city's skyline, sweeping the metropolis in an amber light that signalled the start of a new day and the shedding of an old one. As brightness poured through the giving clouds, the cityscape was bathed in a beautiful blend of pale orange and soft lavender that was reflected in the towering skyscrapers that stretched towards the heavens, as if in an effort to bask in the natural brilliance.

On top of a skyscraper, Simon Jones stood in quiet solitude and contemplation, the events of the previous night lingering in his mind. It had been a successful intervention, one that had thwarted the criminal gang's heist at the orphanage, followed by a harrowing chase that had saved innocent lives from a speeding getaway car. His alter ego, a manifestation of his determination to protect, had prevailed once again. And yet, as the sun's rays illuminated the horizon, a question gnawed at his consciousness: could he continue down this path indefinitely? The question hung in the air like a shroud, tugging at Simon's thoughts as he gazed out over the sprawling cityscape. He had become accustomed to his role as London's silent guardian, a force that stood between chaos and order. But beneath the veneer of strength lay a niggling uncertainty, an uncertainty he couldn't shake.

As his mind wrestled with the weight of his identity, the voice of the Fallen Ring emerged in his thoughts. *How will you answer this question, Simon?* Its cadence was one of counsel and contemplation.

Simon's brows furrowed as he engaged in the internal dialogue, his mind seeking clarity among the complex emotions that churned within him. The Ring's presence had been a constant companion, offering advice and insight born from an existence spanning multiple millennia. And yet, as he contemplated his future, he wondered whether he could truly lay down the mantle of the vigilante he had become.

Taking a break, even temporarily, might be wise, the Ring's voice continued, its tone a mixture of encouragement and reflection. *You have given much to this city, Simon. Your journey towards redemption has been marked by your actions, and perhaps it is time to consider what lies beyond.*

Simon continued to stare down upon the city below, its streets teeming with life and stories yet to be written. A life less burdened, a life in which he could share his days with Layla without the constant tug of the duties of his alter ego was an attractive proposition. It was a concept that held both allure and anxiety – a crossroads where his identity as a protector and his desire for a normal existence converged.

'But could I truly step away?' Simon's thoughts spilled forth as he voiced his inner conflict. 'Could I leave behind this life, even with all its challenges and sacrifices?'

The Ring's voice resonated in his mind. *The path you choose is yours alone, Simon. I offer counsel, but the decisions that shape your destiny rest within you. We've been together long enough for me to trust your judgement.*

Simon mused over the Ring's words, a sense of resolution settling within him. The time had come to reveal his alter ego to Layla, a disclosure that carried considerable uncertainty and vulnerability. It would be a step towards a new equilibrium, a bridge between his dual identities.

A faint smile touched Simon's lips as he envisioned the conversations and revelations that lay ahead. He imagined Layla's reaction, the mingling of surprise, concern and understanding that would inevitably accompany the unveiling of his secret. And through it all, he hoped for the strength to convey his intentions: to explore a life that balanced his commitment to justice with a life that retained some normalcy.

His contemplation was broken by a familiar sound. He reached into his pocket and retrieved the ringing phone. The caller ID displayed his mother's name.

'Hey, Mum.'

'Simon, dear, I hope I'm not interrupting anything.' Her voice was warm and comforting.

Simon's lips curved into a reassuring smile. 'Not at all, Mum. What's up?'

'Could you do me a favour, sweetheart? We're having a gathering at the house later, and I realised we're running low on drinks. Could you pick up a few things on your way back?'

Simon chuckled softly, the mundanity of the request grounding him completely from the currents of his contemplation. 'Of course, Mum. Anything specific you need?'

A list of items followed, each word spoken with a mother's love and attention to detail. As the conversation drew to a close, Simon's thoughts lingered on the task at hand. There was a sense of comfort in the mundane, a reminder that life's moments were composed of both extraordinary challenges and ordinary joys.

'I've got it, Mum. I'll see you soon,' he said with a cheerful smile.

Sliding his phone back into his pocket, he took a final look at the city spread out before him. The path ahead remained unknown, but in that moment, as he descended from the skyscraper and back into the embrace of the waking world, he carried a sense of purpose, one that extended beyond the shadow he cast as a vigilante.

For Simon, London's silent protector, was on the precipice of a new chapter – one that would hopefully blend the extraordinary with the everyday.

Chapter 8

The sun's sweltering heat bore down upon the deserts of Egypt, the vast expanse of golden sand stretching as far as the eye could see. Overlooking this arid realm stood Eradax, the alien being whose iron-like form gleamed in the relentless sunlight. His fiery yellow eyes blazed with an intensity that mirrored the inferno of his purpose. Before him, the majestic pyramids rose from the earth, their ancient stones steeped in mystery and whispers of bygone eras. Eradax's presence cast a shadow upon the landscape, an omen that signified the weight of his quest – a quest that spanned tens of thousands of years, driven by one mad desire.

The hieroglyphics etched into the pyramids bore secrets that were known to only a few, but beneath Eradax's gaze, their meaning unravelled. His existence, marked by many millennia of watching the world, had gifted him with a profound understanding of languages long extinct, echoes of civilisations erased by time. The glyphs revealed the truth he sought; the technological device capable of harnessing the cosmos lay not within the pyramids themselves but buried deep beneath the sands that cradled the ancient structures. Eradax's determination surged as he set his course. The earth's embrace would yield to his will, its layers offering passage to the relic that had eluded him for an eternity.

Raising his hand, Eradax made a series of intricate gestures, before opening his palm, to which the earth quivered in response, the sands parting as a chasm yawned before him. The ground trembled beneath his feet as he descended into the depths, the layers of earth and rock giving way to his advance.

As Eradax ventured deeper, through strata and sediment, the world around him transformed. His fiery gaze pierced through layers of time, remnants of civilisations long forgotten by those who still walked upon the earth's surface. The journey was relentless, a descent that led him through the crust and mantle, where heat and pressure reigned supreme. The searing conditions tore at him, the onslaught relentless, enveloping him. Pain gripped him, overwhelming his senses, trapping him. But he continued undeterred, his form resistant to forces that should have consumed him, the pain a mere phase, and one from which he grew in strength. Anger, hatred and resentment sharpened his resolve, the earth yielding to his presence, its very essence cowering before his rageful might.

The outer core lay before him, a maelstrom of molten metal that churned with an intensity that mirrored Eradax's own fervent drive. He navigated the fiery currents, his form unyielding as he traversed the blistering domain that remained hidden from human eyes.

Reaching the heart of the core's tumultuous embrace, he saw it. The relic he sought, the Infinity Forge, rested within, its ancient visage untouched by the clock of time.

Eradax took a step towards the ancient artefact, his eyes gleaming with anticipation, his outstretched hand inches away from claiming it. But just as he was about to make contact, the walls of the cavern began to tremble and distort, the earth seeming to rise up against him. From the scorching mantle emerged two colossal beings, their forms chiselled from jagged stone and solidified magma. The guardians, silent sentinels of the relic's sanctuary, stood tall and imposing, their expressions carvings of unwavering resolve, the ultimate protectors of a power that should remain undisturbed.

Eradax felt his patience wane as he regarded the guardians. He did not appreciate the sudden interference and had no time for a pathetic quibble. With an air of disdain, he addressed the towering figures.

'I have no patience for this, and certainly none for you. Stand aside, and perhaps I will spare your lives.'

But the guardians did not waver.

'It is our solemn duty to protect the Infinity Forge', replied one of the towering rock figures, its stony features unmoving, 'and we shall not yield, trespasser.'

Eradax scoffed at the guardian's proclamation. 'Fools. You serve a purpose you cannot comprehend. You are mere puppets in an ancient game of power, and the powers that placed you in this role have no care for you. You are nothing but minions to their whims.'

In swift response, the guardians produced halberd polearms, their angular forms gleaming in the cavern as the giants primed themselves, ready to attack.

Eradax's dark laughter filled the cavern as he held aloft his hand which transformed into a wickedly sharp broadsword. He assumed a battle-ready posture, his tusks extending and interlocking, forming a menacing faceplate. 'If you dare to challenge me, then so be it. Through bloodshed we shall discover who will stand victorious.'

The ensuing battle was a clash of colossal might and sheer brutality. The guardians fought dutifully, their polearms a formidable defence against the intruder. But Eradax possessed an unrivalled force that stemmed from his history and dogged determination. He moved with deadly precision, his broadsword cutting through the air and striking one of the guardians. The colossal being howled as the blade impaled its stony form, sending a shower of magma-like sparks into the air. The second guardian, undeterred by its companion's fate, lunged at Eradax. But he responded swiftly, catching the guardian's head in a powerful grip and wrenching it from its body. A sickening, earth-shattering crack filled the cavern as the guardian's life-force was torn from it.

Eradax stood triumphant as the lifeless forms of the guardians crumbled to the ground, a tinge of regret passing over his features. 'There was a time when I once would have called you brothers.' He sighed. 'But no more.'

He looked back towards the relic, now more determined to claim it. But his attention was drawn to an ominous rumbling beneath him. The earth quivered, and the echoes of a greater presence reverberated through the cavern, one greater than the guardians he had just faced. In intense anticipation, Eradax watched as the ground cracked and split around his feet. Massive chunks of rock churned and rose as if summoned by an irresistible force. This was no ordinary occurrence; it was the awakening of a monumental guardian, a being born from the very bedrock of the earth. But the transformation was slow and deliberate, the stony components melding together as nature itself sculpted this behemoth. Each movement, each piece of its massive form, carried an almost divine weight. The ground quaked, and Eradax took a large step back. He was about to face something far more formidable than the previous guardians.

As the final piece locked into place, the gargantuan guardian stood tall and unmoving, its sheer size dwarfing the earlier guardians. It held a colossal sword in one hand and an enormous shield in the other. Eradax, despite his own imposing presence, appeared insignificant before this gigantic figure.

Eradax locked eyes with the guardian, standing tall and unyielding. He regarded his newly arisen adversary with awe and defiance. The guardian's voice reverberated, its words heavy with the weight of centuries.

'Eradax, this is as far as you come. Turn back now, for you have been banished!'

The voice echoed within Eradax's thoughts, its resonance seeking to affect his will. But Eradax remained steadfast, his unblinking eyes unwavering. Like a fiery tempest, his rage began to rise.

'Eradax ... is commanded by no one!' he roared in defiance, his voice echoing throughout the cavern, challenging the guardian's authority.

The guardian responded with chilling resolve: 'As you wish.'

With that, the colossal guardian raised its sword, casting a daunting shadow over Eradax. The enormous blade descended with overwhelming force, aiming to cleave Eradax in two.

Eradax's chest pounded with fierce determination. In an instant, wings sprouted from his back, lifting him into the air. His movements were swift and agile as he dodged the sweeping arc of the guardian's sword. In a moment of daring, Eradax swooped beneath a subsequent strike, the air howling past him. Gathering momentum, he banked sharply, the fiery energy in his fist intensifying. Then, like a comet's descent, Eradax hurtled towards the guardian. His iron-clad fist collided with the titan's face, the impact sending shockwaves like an earthquake across Egypt and the rest of the Middle East and North Africa. Time seemed to slow, the echo of the strike reverberating through the cavern. The guardian's form fractured, a network of cracks racing across its stony visage, and fragments cascaded to the ground as the colossal figure crumbled.

Landing before the fallen behemoth, Eradax retracted his wings into the iron-clad carapace of his body, a victorious sigh escaping his lips as he surveyed the rubble. 'You are far from the last to suffer my wrath.'

With the path now clear of obstruction, he returned his focus to the Infinity Forge and stepped towards it and traced his fingers across its surface. The ancient relic was a testament to a past that had been relegated to obscurity, an artefact of a civilisation that had wielded power far beyond human comprehension, far beyond anything humans could ever engineer. Its intricate design was of an era where the boundaries between science, magic and the chemistry of the cosmos blurred, when the potential of the universe could be harnessed and contained within the device's sophisticated form.

Eradax's iron-like fingers closed around the Infinity Forge, a surge of energy coursing through his being. He could sense its capability to reshape the universe – but also to wipe it out. It pulsed with a resonance that echoed across the dimensions, a power that transcended the barriers of the physical realm. It was a conduit to the very beginning of time. As his grip tightened, his consciousness merged with the ancient wisdom of the relic. The memories of a civilisation that had risen and fallen before humanity had taken its first steps flooded his mind: a spectacle of ambition, discovery and ultimate dissolution.

Eradax's fiery eyes blazed with an insane intensity. He had journeyed through the vast voids of space to claim what he sought. To fulfil his promise to the ancients. To the Superlunary Ones. And to himself. The relic was the key to his ultimate goal – a universal reality devoid of all existence.

With a purpose that burned brighter than the sun, Eradax lifted the Infinity Forge high above his head, its brilliance casting an eerie glow upon the depths of the Earth's core, an alien being harnessing a power that had lain dormant for multiple millennia.

'I've longed for this, and I will soon have what I desire,' he declared.

His triumph was reflected in a symphony of echoes. It was a force that would realise his frightening ambition.

Chapter 9

The cavern echoed with the weight of Eradax's steps as he advanced towards the tunnel he had burrowed, the relic cradled securely in his grasp. Now in possession of what he had come for, it was time to leave.

But as he picked his way towards the entrance, a subtle shift in the shadows pricked at his senses. A pair of crimson eyes gleamed softly from the inky blackness, a sinister sign of the presence concealed within the darkness.

Eradax tilted his head to one side, recognition flickering within his calculating gaze. It couldn't be ... 'You?' he intoned, his voice a blend of surprise and apprehension.

Emerging from the obscurity, the mysterious figure revealed himself: a man with unruly curls of ginger, shrouded in a dark cloak. The man's lips curved into a sardonic smile as he acknowledged Eradax's astonishment. 'Yes, it is I ... Surprised to see me?'

Eradax stood firm, his eyes boring into the man, probing his intentions. The revelation came swiftly, knowledge cascading through his consciousness in a sudden downpour. It was him, the embodiment of deception, the whisperer of temptations, the master of illusions – the Prince of Darkness himself.

The ginger-haired figure gestured towards the relic cradled in Eradax's hand, his tone uncomfortably curious. 'You've done it. I must admit, I did not anticipate this. I can only wonder at what you have in mind.'

'Indeed. However, I have no business with you,' Eradax declared, staring into the man's eyes, his focus steadfast.

The cloaked man's countenance contorted with a mixture of astonishment and vexation. 'You cannot be serious. There's more to be gained here. Don't you realise?'

Without a second glance, Eradax turned and strode away, his purpose unwavering.

The cloaked man's voice cut through the cavern's solemnity once more, urgent and persuasive. 'Eradax, you underestimate what is within your grasp. You do not need the Infinity Forge when I can grant you everything you want. Just tell me.'

At those words, Eradax halted. Slowly, he turned to face the fork-tongued man, his eyes burning with a fierce intensity. 'You can offer me nothing,' he declared with resolute conviction. 'You too are a pawn in this grand scheme, offering mere illusions. And I am in need of none. If you were to grant me anything though, I would wish for your demise!'

Eradax's words hung heavy in the air, his eyes boring into the ginger-haired man's very essence. 'I warn you, do not cross my path again.'

With that final statement, Eradax resumed his stride, leaving the cloaked man alone in the darkness. The once-smiling figure, now stripped of mirth, looked on, a mask of stunned disbelief settling over his features.

Chapter 10

Eradax ascended from the depths, his iron-clad form radiating with the energy of ancient power. In his grasp, the Infinity Forge, an artefact of forgotten eras, pulsated with a vibration that mirrored the hidden rhythms of the universe. The sands of Egypt whispered as the winds carried the echoes of his purpose.

With a drive as immutable as the stars themselves, Eradax rose to the precipice of the burrow and stepped out. The chasm closed in his wake, leaving no trace of his passage, no indication of the perilous journey he had undertaken, nor the battles he had just fought. His fiery yellow eyes blazed with determination as he contemplated the path that lay ahead. The relic was a piece of the puzzle, a key that unlocked the potential to reshape the cosmos itself. But to harness its true power, he needed the other piece of the puzzle – a Fallen Ring – another conduit of authority that would unlock the relic's true potential.

As Eradax set his sights on his new goal, his thoughts drifted back through the annals of time, to a history marked by servitude. He had been a herald for the Superlunary Ones, entities that stood just beneath the Cosmic

Being in the hierarchy of the universe. Their command had been his directive, their whims his reality. But as the universe expanded and life flourished across the tapestry of the world, he had grappled with questions that transcended his purpose; the futility of existence – the cycle of birth, life and death – had gnawed at his soul. The concept of following orders without question, of existing solely to submit, had ignited a spark of rebellion within him.

He had dared to question the Superlunary Ones, to voice his discontent and to seek understanding of the laws of the cosmos. Why had such a vast universe been created, one full of constant contradictions? Why had choice been limited? If fate was real, then was free will merely an illusion? When would it all end? Their responses had been enigmatic, laden with cryptic wisdom that both intrigued and infuriated him. And then came the ultimate decree: a verdict that had cast him out as a renegade, a pariah banished to the farthest reaches of the galaxy.

Eradax looked up to the sky, his fiery eyes tracing the constellations that adorned the galaxies above. His voice had been silenced, his place among the Superlunary Ones usurped by the echoes of his supposed defiance. He had been cast into the cold abyss of isolation, and no one had reached out to him. Neither to save him nor to make things right. It was this solitary existence that had fuelled his determination to destroy them – and the universe. He had walked the path of servitude and been cast aside as a rebel, and now he stood poised to enact his ultimate vision: a vision born from a belief that life's purpose extended beyond the constraints of cosmic hierarchy. He had woken up to see the façade of existence for what it was and would no longer let it be. With the contours of the Fallen Ring in his thoughts, Eradax strengthened his resolve. No force would deter him. No power would halt his ascent.

He drew his attention back to his earthly surroundings. The two relics together held the promise of a cataclysmic transformation. He would be able to unlock the Infinity Forge's true power, a power that would catalyse the erasure of everything that existed – all that was, all that is and all that would be.

The universe itself seemed to hold its breath, the threads of destiny weaving towards the nexus of his intent. Eradax was no longer a herald or a renegade; he was an architect of annihilation, a force that would extinguish life's fragile flame before extinguishing his own. His mission was the ultimate act. An act that no being had ever conceived. It was the supreme decision. For the fate of all things would come by his hand. He would see to it.

It was at that moment that Eradax recalled a saying he had heard some years ago: 'Not all monsters are born, some are created. Yet so many of those who hold responsibility always choose to deny such truth. That is until they are forced to watch on as their creation shows them what a real monster is capable of. Then, when the dust settles and the Armageddon has died down, they may just realise, that for creating such a monster, there are consequences to follow.'

Chapter 11

The sun painted the sky with hues of gold and amber, casting a warm glow over the city as Simon and Layla walked together. Their steps falling in sync, he glanced over at her, smiling inwardly. These quiet moments with her were increasingly becoming a treasured part of his day. Moments of simple togetherness meant more to him than he could put into words.

His life hadn't been an easy one: the people he had lost, the criminals he had killed, the enemies he had made, the months of estrangement and loneliness, his night life as a vigilante, always looking over his shoulder. Despite his accomplishments, he was still asserting his place in the wider world, figuring out what his priorities were and what he could achieve with his powers. Sometimes it was all a bit much. But Layla's presence was a balm to soothe his troubles. With her by his side, he felt more grounded, more at peace than he had in earlier times.

The thrill of patrolling the city would never lose its appeal. There was a rush that came with using his abilities, communicating with the Ring in his mind and being instrumental in keeping the streets safe. But it was still a fairly solitary existence, one that tended to be harsher and less forgiving. Layla represented the softer parts of life that he had long neglected: companionship, tenderness, someone to come home to. He had grown close to Layla over the years, building a relationship of trust, honesty and commitment.

The conversation between them flowed effortlessly, a mosaic of topics from Simon's new job at the cybersecurity firm to Layla's own job interviews. They spoke of aspirations and dreams, sharing their hopes for the future as their footsteps carried them through the city centre.

'Speaking of the future', Layla began, a glint of mischief in her eyes, 'my family is planning a get-together later this year. They can't wait to have you over again.'

Simon chuckled, the prospect of seeing Layla's family was both exciting and nerve-wracking. 'I'm sure it'll be loads of fun. Besides, remember what happened last time we ate dinner?'

Layla laughed. 'Yeah, I remember. You butchered the roast turkey. Even my mum couldn't stop laughing. I hope you're prepared for even more food.'

Simon chuckled, his heart swelling with affection, the funny memory still fresh in his mind. But despite his laughter and the beautiful day around them, something didn't feel quite right. He glanced at Layla, who appeared relaxed and happy as she started on another story. Tightening his grip on her hand as they entered a park, he scanned their surroundings, his senses on the alert. But as they turned down onto a small path, two thugs appeared before them, blocking the way ahead. The sagging pants of the thugs and their confrontational stances exuded an air of menace. Layla instinctively moved closer to Simon as he took the lead.

'If you want to pass, you got to pay us a fee, mate,' demanded the thug in front, his outstretched hand a sign of his overconfidence.

'Not today, mate,' Simon said, refusing the demand. He attempted to steer Layla away, to sidestep the confrontation, but the bullies persisted, their intentions clear.

A shove from one of the thugs set Simon off, his reflexes surging into life. In an instant, he twisted the first thug's hand with practised precision, the man's yelp of pain punctuating the air as he fell to his knees. The second thug hesitated, then, with his resolve crumbling like sand between fingers, he turned and fled the scene. Scrambling to his feet, the first thug scarpered after him, cradling his injured hand.

Layla's eyes widened, a mixture of shock and admiration painted across her features. She stared at Simon, probing him for answers. 'Did you ... do karate or something?' Her voice was tinged with curiosity and awe.

Simon met her gaze, his eyes harbouring the secret he had long kept hidden. He offered a half-smile, a mask that concealed the truth that rested beneath the surface. 'Err ... I did, actually,' he replied cryptically.

She linked her arm with his. 'Well, it's a good thing I have you. I don't know what I would have done by myself.'

Simon's heart swelled with pride and happiness. Layla was his beacon of light in a world that had often been shrouded in darkness. He cherished these moments, the ordinary yet extraordinary interactions that defined their connection.

As they continued their leisurely walk, the Ring's voice resurfaced in Simon's mind. *Will you reveal your secret? Will you trust her with this revelation?* It was a choice that could forever alter the course of his life. Simon's thoughts churned, the weight of his secret a burden that had grown heavier each time he decided not to speak of it.

He glanced at Layla, her smile radiating a warmth that thawed the walls around his heart. The words of the Ring echoed in his mind, urging him to consider the possibility of unveiling his truth. Could he trust Layla with the knowledge of his alter ego? What would she say if he told her about the power that coursed through his veins?

A moment of vulnerability washed over him, the realisation that his relationship with Layla deserved this level of honesty. The words of the Ring became a resolute conviction, an affirmation that the time had come to share his secret – a secret that defined his nights and shaped much of his purpose.

Coming to a stop, Simon drew in a deep breath as he turned to face Layla, his heart racing as he steeled himself to bridge the gap between his two worlds. He looked into her eyes, a wellspring of emotions swirling within their depths as she looked back at him with amused curiosity. He opened his mouth to speak, the weight of the truth poised on the precipice of revelation.

Chapter 12

Simon's heart continued to race as he looked into Layla's eyes, a mixture of apprehension and determination swirling within him. The weight of his secret, carried for so long, rested heavy upon his shoulders. A cool breeze from the nearby water brushed against his skin, bringing his attention back to Layla, who was starting to look slightly concerned. He must seize the moment. It was time to reveal his alter ego, his nights spent as the Elusive Guardian of the city.

'Layla,' he began, his voice tinged with vulnerability, 'there's something I need to tell you. Something I should have told you a while ago.'

Layla's brows furrowed slightly, her gaze unwavering. 'What is it, Simon?'

He took her hand in his, his grip steady despite the turmoil within him. 'Follow me, I'll show you.'

Guiding her through the bustling streets of Central London, he felt removed from the people around, his mind buzzing with a mix of anticipation and anxiety. He led Layla to a more secluded area near the docks, where the gentle lapping of the water against the quayside provided a soothing backdrop.

Standing overlooking the water, he searched for the right words, his throat suddenly dry. 'Layla,' he said, turning to face her, 'what I'm about to tell you might be hard to believe, but I need you to trust me.'

Layla nodded, her eyes fixed on his. 'Simon, you know you can tell me anything. I trust you.'

He drew in a deep breath. 'I'm not just an ordinary guy, Layla. By day I'm Simon Jones, the guy who just graduated, who works a regular job. But at night I become someone else. Something else. Something that roams the city's shadows, that fights crime and helps those in need.'

Layla's eyes widened. 'What are you saying, Simon? Are you some kind of vigilante?'

Simon nodded, the weight of his revelation palpable. 'Yes, that's exactly it. At night I become the one that the city calls the Elusive Guardian.'

Layla's breath caught as she struggled with the revelation. 'You mean ... all those stories about the mysterious protector ... it's you?'

Simon nodded again, his heart pounding in his chest. 'I didn't want to keep this from you, Layla. But I was afraid how you'd react.'

Layla's expression shifted from surprise to a mixture of concern and intrigue. 'I-I don't know what to say ... this is a lot to take in.'

Simon took a step closer, his eyes searching hers. 'Layla, please understand that I've only been doing this to make the city safer. With the powers I have, it felt like the right thing to do.'

Layla's eyes softened, a smile tugging at the corners of her lips. 'You've been risking your life to protect others?'

Simon smiled shyly, his heart warmed by Layla's compassion. 'Yes. And now that you know, I hope you can see why I couldn't keep this from you any longer.'

Layla's smile broadened, a playful glint in her eyes. 'You know, this is like something out of a film. Who'd have thought it? I'm in a relationship with a superhero?'

Simon chuckled, his tension easing at Layla's light-hearted response. 'I promise you, it's not as glamorous as it sounds.'

'So, how does it all work? said Layla, her head tilting to one side. 'How did you get these abilities?'

Simon reached into his pocket and pulled out the silver Ring. 'It all started with this,' he said, holding it up for Layla to see. 'This Ring, it's not just an ordinary piece of jewellery. It's ancient and powerful and the source of my powers.'

Layla studied the intricate runes etched on the Ring's surface. 'It's beautiful ... and it's the reason you can do what you do?'

Simon nodded, a mixture of gratitude and responsibility coursing through him. 'Yes. The Ring grants me enhanced speed, strength and a plethora of other abilities. With these powers, I've been able to make a difference.'

Layla's eyes gleamed with wonder. 'Can I see it in action? Can you show me?'

Simon hesitated as he considered the request. 'Of course, but maybe we should find a more secluded—'

Before he could finish his sentence, a sudden blast of energy struck him, knocking him off his feet, sending him several feet into the air before he hit the ground with a painful thud. Layla's scream echoed in his ears as she rushed to his side, concern etched across her face.

'Simon! Are you okay?' Layla's voice trembled as she knelt beside him, her hands gently checking him for injuries.

Simon groaned, his body aching from the impact. He pushed himself up onto his elbows, his senses reeling from the unexpected attack. 'I ... I'm fine, just a bit shaken.' He looked up and smiled in an effort to reassure Layla, but her eyes were wide with fear as she stared beyond him, her face drained of all colour. As he turned and looked over his shoulder, his heart froze in his chest.

Hovering above the water was an alien being. Its skin, which resembled iron, was etched with intricate designs that seemed to shift and writhe in the light, its fiery yellow eyes fixated on Simon, the weight of its piercing glare heavy and unnerving.

Simon's mind slipped into sixth gear, his heart pounding as he tried to make sense of the situation. Who – or what – was this being? Why had it attacked him?

As the being touched down on the ground, the air around them crackled with electricity. Simon's body tensed, his instincts on high alert. Layla clung to his side, her fear palpable as they faced this mysterious and formidable adversary.

CHAPTER 13

Eradax stood tall and imposing, his iron-clad skin gleaming in the ambient light. His fiery yellow eyes bore into the figure before him, assessing him with a mixture of curiosity and disdain. The energy of the attack, which still lingered in the air, spoke of his mighty power. Looking at the young man, he couldn't help but marvel at the fact that this seemingly ordinary human possessed the coveted Fallen Ring.

'Young man,' Eradax began, his voice carrying an air of authority, 'I apologise for the late introduction. I am Eradax.'

Simon rose to his feet, his posture defiant, and met Eradax's scrutiny head on. 'Eradax? What kind of name is that?'

Eradax's mouth curled into a subtle smile. 'A name that holds power, significance and the promise of colossal cosmic change. I've come for the Fallen Ring. Give it to me, and we can avoid a potential calamity.'

'Never!' Simon declared, his tone resolute. 'I don't know who you are or how you found me, but you're not getting this Ring.'

Eradax's patience waned, his blazing eyes narrowing. 'Very well then. If you insist on resisting, I shall take it by force.'

With a swift motion, Eradax summoned another dark energy blast, sending it hurtling towards the young man. But in a display of remarkable agility, Simon dodged the discharge as his form shifted and transformed. His entire being became cloaked in a dark-purple aura, a symbol of the power he also possessed. Shielding himself from the blast, he wrapped a muscle-bound arm around Layla and pulled her into his side.

'Go!' he urged in her ear, his voice commanding and urgent.

Pulling away from him, Layla began to stagger away.

With a wicked grin, Eradax feigned his aim at the purple humanoid before turning his hand towards the young woman and blasting a beam of explosive energy towards her.

The shockwave of the blast caught her, knocking her back, and Layla stumbled and collapsed to the ground, her breath shallow as she struggled to regain her senses.

The purple Guardian stepped towards Layla, concern and anger warring in his eyes as she lay there, barely conscious. Turning his attention back to Eradax, the Guardian's eyes blazed with infuriation, sending a twinge of unease through Eradax. The purple vigilante wasn't about to back down.

'Fighting back, are we?' Eradax sneered, his metallic skin reflecting the ominous glow of the purple energy before him.

The Guardian's response was swift and fierce. With a powerful leap, he lunged at Eradax, his fists striking with incredible force, each blow resonating like a thunderclap.

Finding himself on the defensive, Eradax fought back, activating his tusks to shield himself and counterattacking, his iron fists connecting with the dark-purple humanoid, sending shockwaves of energy rippling through the air. The clash between them was intense, both combatants pushing their limits as they battled for supremacy.

Yet, with every blow that Eradax landed, he realised that the purple Guardian's strength and resilience were greater than he had anticipated. The tables had turned. He was facing an adversary who refused to surrender. Blow after blow, the Guardian's unwavering determination fuelled his strikes, driving Eradax to the brink of frustration.

A devastating uppercut from the Guardian sent Eradax hurtling backwards, bringing their confrontation to its zenith, the force of the blow propelling Eradax into the waters of the dock with a resounding splash. As the water cascaded around him, Eradax's rage burned hotter than ever before. Emerging from the water, his fiery eyes blazing, Eradax roared with inflamed fury. He scanned the area, his gaze narrowing. The purple humanoid and the young woman were nowhere to be found.

'You may have escaped for now,' Eradax growled, his voice carrying across the water, 'but you cannot hide from me forever. I will have the Fallen Ring!'

His resolve unshaken, Eradax's energy surged, shattering the windows in the buildings, and bringing down the nearby cranes. As he turned and levitated away, a plethora of onlookers gaped in awe and terror at the destruction that lay in his wake.

The power of the young man's alter ego might have frustrated the course of his grand plan, but that mattered little. He would not underestimate him a second time.

Chapter 14

The city's skyline rushed by in a blur of lights and shadows as Simon carried Layla through the late afternoon, his heart pounding with a mix of urgency and worry. The weight of her body in his arms felt heavier with each passing second, a constant reminder of the danger they had faced.

His thoughts raced, questions spiralling through his mind like a whirlwind. Who was Eradax? And why had he targeted them? How had he known about the power of the Fallen Ring? And – most importantly – what were his intentions?

His leaps and bounds carried them closer to the hospital, the beacon of hope that he desperately needed in this dire moment. He could feel Layla's shallow breaths against his chest, her feeble voice calling out his name. Gently, he adjusted his hold on her, his expression full of pain and concern. 'Hang on, Layla. We're almost there.'

As the hospital's towering façade grew closer, Simon halted on a rooftop just outside, his pulse racing as he carefully laid Layla down.

She looked up at him, her eyes struggling to focus as she whispered, 'What ... happened?'

Simon's voice was soothing and laced with a touch of relief. 'You got hurt, but you're safe now. I'm going to get you the help you need.'

Layla managed a weak smile, her fingers brushing against his hand. 'That's ... good to know.'

The silver Ring on his finger pulsed with a gentle warmth as a healing energy flowed into Layla. The Ring's voice echoed in his mind, reassuring him that the transfer would aid in Layla's recovery. As a faint colour returned to her cheeks, Simon's racing heart eased slightly.

Cradling Layla in his arms once more, Simon descended from the rooftop and raced to the hospital entrance. Swiftly, he transformed back into his normal self, the dark-purple shroud receding back into the Ring. As he entered the hospital's bustling reception area, emergency personnel hurried over, their trained eyes assessing the situation, taking charge. Simon's voice was steady as he provided Layla's details, ensuring that they had his contact information for updates on her condition. The medical team whisked Layla away as he watched on anxiously, his thoughts turning to his past, to the best friend he had lost years ago – James. The memory of that loss weighed heavily upon him, a reminder of the fragility of life and the lengths he would go to protect those he cared about.

In the dimly lit hospital corridor, Simon leaned against the wall, his chest tightening with a flurry of emotions. He clenched his fists, the cool metal of the Fallen Ring pressing into his palm. He couldn't let history repeat itself.

He couldn't lose another person who meant so much to him. This lingering fear gnawed at the edge of his thoughts – the fear of losing Layla, just as he had lost James.

As the minutes ticked by, Simon's mind raced with dread. Their encounter with Eradax had thrust them into a dangerous battle, one that he needed to face head on. With each passing moment, his determination solidified, his heart and mind aligning in a fierce vow. He would do whatever it would take to ensure Layla's safety, to protect her from the impending threat that loomed over them. He had no choice.

With the hospital buzzing with activity around him, Simon's eyes remained fixed on the corridor down which Layla had been taken. His fingers traced the contours of the Fallen Ring, a symbol of not only his power but also his tenacity. The echoes of past losses reverberated within him, fuelling a fire that burned brighter than ever.

Chapter 15

Echoes of Layla's weak voice lingered in Simon's mind as he walked through the busy streets of London. All around him, news of the alien attack at the docks filled the digital screens and TVs; there were even a few photos of his purple alter ego. People were huddled around the screens, eager to know more about the horrifying event. Seeing this, he boiled with anger, a seething rage consuming his thoughts. How dare that alien being attack Layla! What if his secret identity had been uncovered? It had threatened everything that he held dear.

With his fists clenched at his sides, fury simmered within his chest. Every step he took resonated with the promise he had made to himself: he would tear Eradax's head from his body if Layla didn't make it.

Yet, the throbbing pain in parts of his body served as a stark reminder of the power wielded by the alien being. He winced, remembering the blows that had struck him with an unearthly force. He had been lucky in that initial confrontation – and he knew it.

As he strode onwards, his thoughts began to shift, branching into the realisation that he couldn't face this threat alone. He needed more than just his own abilities; he needed help, strength beyond measure. And as unsettling as it was, an idea began to take root: perhaps it was time to call upon an old enemy, a rival who had once posed a significant threat.

Simon's footsteps faltered as he considered the implications of his decision. The risks and danger of reaching out to someone who had once been his adversary were serious. But the threat at hand was far greater. The alien being who sought the Fallen Ring had spoken of wanting 'colossal cosmic change'.

His mind settled on the name – Viktor Nemesis – a name that carried the scars of past battles and a rivalry that he would never forget. Simon's eyes darkened as he contemplated the path he was about to tread. Could he trust Viktor? Could he rely on him to fight in a battle that would transcend their personal vendettas?

With a heavy sigh, Simon acknowledged that he had little choice. Eradax's power was indeed significant and facing him alone would be disastrous. There was only one course of action. He would have to venture into the Shadow Plane, the realm where Viktor had been confined.

An empty alley provided the perfect cover for Simon's abilities. Closing his eyes, he focused on the power of the Fallen Ring that flowed through him. Slowly, a rip in reality began to form before him, a portal to the shadowy realm that existed beyond the bounds of the physical world. As the portal grew larger, its edges shimmering with an otherworldly hue, Simon steeled himself for what lay ahead, his heart racing with apprehension. This was a gamble, a risky move born out of necessity. With a final glance back at the world he knew, he took a deep breath and stepped into the void – and into a different world.

The decision had been made. It was too late to go back on it now.

CHAPTER 16

The transition was disorienting, a kaleidoscope of darkness and elusive shapes, and the air seemed to hum with an eerie energy, as if the very fabric of the realm recognised Simon's presence. When the dizzying whirlwind subsided, he found himself standing in the shadows of a landscape that was a distorted reflection of the world he had left behind, where reality wavered and twisted. He took a deep breath, his resolve firm. It was time to face Viktor Nemesis. The encounter would be a delicate balance of negotiation and risk. Their past and Viktor's own motivations would collide, and only time would tell whether an alliance could be forged against the impending cosmic threat. The path was perilous, the stakes were high and the line between ally and enemy was blurred in this twilight realm. Yet, for the sake of Layla, his family and the city he had vowed to protect, he was willing to venture into the heart of darkness itself.

As he moved forward, each step seemed to echo with a soft whisper, as if the shadows held secrets he had yet to uncover. His heart raced, the anticipation of what lay ahead mingling with a sense of unease. Yet, purpose propelled his steps.

Nearing some buildings, he sensed a familiar energy nearby, the presence he was seeking in this desolate place. The shadows cast haunting patterns across his path as he followed the pull of energy, guided by intuition from his Ring. He came to a standstill before a derelict, inky building that seemed to absorb all light, leaving behind a bleak contrast of grey and black shadows. He hesitated for a moment, his gaze sweeping across the ominous structure. This was the place. This is where he believed he would find Viktor. Taking a steadying breath, he crossed the threshold into the building. The interior was as devoid of colour as the exterior: a monochromatic wasteland where shadows clung to every surface. The air was heavy, the silence punctuated only by his footsteps echoing against the walls.

In the midst of the desolation sat a man, his tattered clothing blending seamlessly with his bleak surroundings. His dark hair and beard were unkempt, and a slight air of frenzy clung to him.

Simon's eyes narrowed as he approached, his heart quickening as recognition set in. 'Viktor Nemesis,' he called out, his voice echoing through the desolate chamber.

The man's head lifted, his eyes locking onto Simon's with a glint of recognition. A memory seemed to flicker within those dark-blue depths, a remnant of their past encounters.

'Simon,' Viktor's voice was hoarse, tinged with fatigue. 'It's been too long, hasn't it? What brings you to this forsaken place? To bask in your victory over your fallen rival?'

Simon shook his head, his gaze unwavering. 'No, you know I'd never come for that,' he replied firmly. 'I need your help, Viktor. A threat has emerged. One that could destroy our very world or plunge it into chaos.'

Viktor responded with a casual shrug and an air of indifference. He appeared unaffected by the impending danger, even for his own well-being, which was an intriguing matter in itself. How had he managed to sustain himself in such a desolate place? That aside, he knew that appealing to Viktor's sense of morality would be futile.

'Your indifference aside, Viktor, cosmic destruction will have serious consequences, even in the Shadow Plane,' Simon said, urgency infiltrating his words. 'The alien force threatening us won't spare anyone. The universe and everything we know is at risk, you included. So, you either stand with me or you succumb to extinction.'

A faint glimmer of intrigue glowed in Viktor's eyes as he contemplated Simon's words, silence stretching between them, each moment laden with the weight of the decision at hand.

Finally, he spoke, his tone begrudging: 'Very well ... I will assist you. But only because this threat could disrupt my existence as well. Once it has been dealt with, our partnership ends. I have no interest in your life or your affairs.'

Simon nodded, accepting Viktor's conditions. The alliance was born out of necessity and not camaraderie. Viktor's motivations remained as self-serving as ever. Still, their combined strength offered the best chance against the alien enemy.

Stepping away momentarily, Simon consulted the silver Ring on his finger. *Can the alien locate us here, in the Shadow Plane?* he asked in his mind.

The Ring's response was a sombre affirmation. *Yes. Eradax is able to track us anywhere.*

Simon's decision was swift. Confronting the alien being in this parallel wasteland was preferable to endangering so many lives in the city. Returning to Viktor's side, he explained his plan, emphasising the need to face the threat in this desolate dimension. Viktor's acceptance was reluctant, a hint of resignation in his eyes.

'Still trying to be goody two shoes aren't you,' Viktor jibed with a sardonic smile.

The tension between them hung heavy, a reminder of the fragile partnership they had formed.

Simon, feeling the pressure of the impending battle, went off to seek a quiet place elsewhere in the building. Finding an empty room that suited his intentions, he sat down in a lotus position and bowed his head, not in submission but in a deliberate act of turning his thoughts inwards. His surroundings faded as he delved into the recesses of his mind.

Rage, a potent force within him, simmered beneath the surface. Instead of suppressing it, Simon allowed it to rise, letting it course through his veins like liquid fire. Anger, once a turbulent force that threatened to consume him, was converted into a controlled energy, and he embraced it, fully present with his emotions, fears and hopes. Not quite meditation, it was more of a rekindling of his strength and focus, harnessing his inner core.

He and Viktor must confront the cosmic threat that loomed large at their door. Their tentative alliance was necessary. Whether it would endure or not remained to be seen. But despite this, they must stand together and face a danger that threatened not only their world but also the very fabric of existence.

CHAPTER 17

Back on Earth, Eradax was standing in a deserted alley, his imposing, alien presence in striking contrast with the mundanity of his surroundings. Fixated on one goal, and one goal only, he studied the device in his hand. The readings on it displayed the energy signature he sought: the resonance of the Fallen Ring's power. Eradax chuckled. Did the boy think he could hide in an alternate dimension? There was nowhere the boy could go that Eradax could not follow. Whatever it took, however long it required, he would see to it that his goal was achieved. The plans were long underway, and there would be no more delays.

Summoning his mystic power, Eradax conjured up his own twisted portal, creating a rift between the dimensions. The portal shimmered before him, a gateway that would lead him from this world to the parallel realm known as the Shadow Plane. Flexing his gargantuan wings, Eradax rose off the ground, his iron-clad skin radiating with an eerie luminescence as he flew through the portal and the fabric of reality closed behind him.

The transition was seamless, as if he had been transported from one world to another in an instant. A triumphant smile spread across his face as he descended upon the barren landscape of the Shadow Plane. He knew he was close to his goal, the Fallen Ring that he sought and the young man who possessed it.

His immense wings beat the air, his large form soaring over the desolate expanse. Around him the sky was a shifting gradient of dark hues and beneath him the ground absorbed any trace of light. As he flew, spectral wraiths flitted below him, lost souls twisted by the very essence of this forsaken dimension. Their pitiable existence reminded him of his own time in exile, a memory he'd never forget.

Guided by the readings from the device, Eradax zeroed in on his target: a figure standing alone amid the desolation, a solitary beacon of life in a sea of shadows. The young man, the bearer of the Fallen Ring, had his back turned to Eradax. It was a bold move, and one that Eradax appreciated. As if the young man actually believed he stood a chance against him. Eradax snorted with derision. The boy had no idea what he had in store for him.

Chapter 18

Eradax's heavy landing was deliberate and dramatic, his feet hitting the ground with a resounding thud as he loomed over the young man, his towering presence casting an ominous shadow over the already ashen soil. His tipped wings retracted into his iron-clad carapace and his laughter echoed through the barren wasteland, taunting the man standing before him.

'You've drawn this out, young one. Especially when you don't have the slightest idea of what is at stake,' Eradax declared. 'The Earth, the world you call home, was founded on deception, yet you defend it. You are young and naive. Despite your powers, you're but a child, whereas I have lived for hundreds of thousands of years, my plans spanning aeons. And you, a mere human, think you can stand in my way?'

The young man locked eyes with his opponent, his shoulders back and his head held high. In a fluid motion, he transformed into the familiar dark-purple humanoid. 'I'm not just standing in your way, Eradax. I'm going to stop you. Once and for all,' he retorted with a sardonic smile.

Eradax's laughter morphed into a malicious grin. 'You speak bravely, but bravery alone cannot save you, child, for I am beyond that now. I ... am the end.'

Eradax had barely finished speaking when a powerful force struck him from behind, and sent him hurtling through the air, crashing into a rugged mountain face. The intensity of the collision sent shockwaves through the rocky terrain as Eradax's iron-clad body smashed into the jagged stone, scattering debris everywhere.

Shaking off the daze of the impact, Eradax pulled himself to his feet and turned and locked onto the source of the attack. Standing next to the purple humanoid was another being, with dark-green skin, fearsome features and a mouth filled with razor-sharp teeth.

The dark-green one grinned slyly. 'Well, well, Eradax, you don't look so tough after that tumble.'

Eradax's eyes sparkled, his smirk returning. 'Two Ring bearers? How intriguing,' he mused, his voice tinged with anticipation. Raising his left arm, he flexed his fingers as they extended to form metallic claws while an extra pair of arms snaked out from his body. 'Get ready to meet your oblivion!' His interlocked tusks glinted menacingly, ready for battle.

Without further hesitation, Eradax lunged forward with incredible speed, his four iron fists aimed at the dark-purple humanoid and the green one. The Ring bearers reacted swiftly, the purple humanoid sidestepping while the green one leaped into the air with surprising agility. Eradax's strikes were swift and precise, but the Ring bearers proved to be formidable opponents. The purple entity showcased incredible acrobatics, using his enhanced speed and strength to weave through Eradax's attacks, countering with well-placed strikes. The dark-green one was no less skilled, using his sharp claws and teeth to tear into Eradax's armour-like skin.

Despite their combined efforts, Eradax's millennia of experience began to tip the scales. He caught the purple humanoid's fist mid-air and twisted it, sending a jolt of pain through the Guardian's arm before wrestling him down and stomping on his back. Clasping the humanoid's chin, Eradax flung him aside. Simultaneously, he dodged a swipe from the green entity and countered with a powerful kick that sent Viktor crashing into a nearby building.

Seeing his companion in trouble, the purple humanoid summoned his chi and unleashed a barrage of energy blasts, forcing Eradax to divert his attention. Seizing the opportunity, the green entity staggered to his feet and lunged at Eradax from behind, sinking his teeth into Eradax's shoulder. Eradax roared in agony, swinging his massive arms and dislodging the dark-green entity, flinging him through the air. The purple humanoid closed in with renewed determination. With a powerful uppercut, he delivered a blow to Eradax's jaw, momentarily staggering him.

Resilient and determined not to be beaten, Eradax recovered quickly, catching the purple humanoid's next punch and retaliating with a brutal knee strike to his midsection, causing a loud crunch. The Guardian gasped for air, his chest heaving heavily. Before he could fully recover, Eradax slammed his iron fists down, creating shockwaves that sent cracks spidering through the ground and forcing the purple humanoid to roll out of harm's way.

The green humanoid rushed in from Eradax's flank and delivered a roundhouse kick to the alien being's left leg before delivering a hook punch to his temple. The purple one followed up with a front kick to Eradax's chest, then a cross punch to his face. Blow by blow, the unlikely partnership fought to break Eradax down, each strike echoing through the shadowy landscape as they fought valiantly, striking simultaneously, but it only lasted so long. Eradax's superior strength and experience were beginning to change the tide of battle.

Evading a tornado kick from the green entity, Eradax caught his leg and slammed him into the dirt before tossing him aside. Countering a haymaker from the purple humanoid, Eradax thrust one of his bladed hands into his abdomen, piercing his adversary with dark delight. With a final, thunderous double punch, Eradax knocked the purple humanoid off his feet and into a multi-storey building, collapsing it and leaving him battered under the rubble.

As Eradax smirked at the decimated structure, a sudden rush of movement came from behind. Before he could react, the dark-green entity lunged at him with a fierce tackle, his momentum driving both of them to the ground. But Eradax would not be so easily overpowered. With a furious snarl, he planted his feet in the dusty soil and pushed against the force of the tackle, halting their momentum. His iron-like muscles strained against the assault as he fought to regain control. Then, seizing the moment, Eradax twisted his body and delivered a devastating body blow to the green humanoid's side and clamped his large hand on his shoulder, crushing his bones and making him cry out in agony. But Eradax wasn't finished yet. With lightning reflexes, he seized the entity by the head and dug his fingers into his skull. A primal scream rang out from the alien as he lifted the dark-green entity off the ground, his raw strength overpowering the struggling beast, and held him high above his head, his eyes burning with vengeful fury. With a mighty roar, he brought the dark-green entity crashing down into the rocky dirt, the ground trembling beneath the force of the impact.

The dark-green entity lay motionless. As he struggled to so much as catch his breath, Eradax towered over him, his chest heaving as he looked down on him with a victorious grin.

'You pathetic mess! Not even the Superlunary Ones can stop me from attaining my destiny,' Eradax declared, his tone dripping with arrogance and elation. 'They, and everyone else, are merely puppets dancing on strings. But no more! For I am no puppet. I ... have no strings.'

Eradax reached out and wrapped his fingers around the green entity's neck and started to squeeze.

The green entity feebly attempted to resist, but the pain was overwhelming.

'You ... have no soul,' the green entity croaked.

'When it was taken from me, I became free. That is why I have no fear!' Eradax replied.

With a swift and determined motion, he yanked the obsidian Ring from the entity's finger, the green glow fading as it was torn away. The dark-green entity's form shifted, reverting to that of a man with long, unkempt hair. The dishevelled man lay shivering on the rocky ground, his breathing laboured and shallow.

Eradax's triumph was palpable. He held the Fallen Ring aloft, his fingers tracing the ancient symbols etched on its surface. An almost emotional connection surged through him. This was a symbol of his victory, a steppingstone towards his ultimate goal. But there was no time for sentimentality. To conquer the future, one must kill the past. His grin widened as his eyes fixed on the relic he had carried with him. With a flick of his wrist, he activated the Infinity Forge, and it began to transform before his eyes. The once small device expanded and morphed into a large, intricate machine. Celestial metal plates shifted and rearranged themselves, forming an intricate structure of crystals, conduits and glowing energy cores. Eradax's eyes gleamed with anticipation as he contemplated the power of the machine, the Fallen Ring clutched tightly in his hand. Eradax positioned the Ring above the machine's receptacle, and a surge of power emanated from within. His heart pounded with the gravity of the moment, and his voice resonated with cold determination.

'I will soon become the One Above All!' he declared, his words echoing through the barren landscape. 'Cosmic annihilation will be my first miracle.'

With a triumphant smile, Eradax lowered the obsidian Ring into the machine's receptacle. A brilliant flash of energy erupted from within, bathing Eradax in an otherworldly light. The machine hummed with power, its energy intertwining with the Ring's ancient magic.

Eradax's grip on the Ring tightened, his whole being consumed by an overwhelming surge of power. His body vibrated with energy, his very essence merging with the immense cosmic forces at play. The machine's humming intensified, resonating with the fabric of reality itself.

Eradax's triumphant grin widened, his eyes blazing with anticipation and an almost maniacal fervour. The machine's energy pulsed and swirled around him, casting shadows against the desolate landscape. The universe held its breath as Eradax stood at the precipice of cosmic devastation, his deadly destiny within reach.

CHAPTER 19

Barely able to move, Viktor Nemesis tilted his head to one side. Standing a little distance away, his new adversary, Eradax, was bent over an otherworldly machine, enacting the final part of his grand scheme. This was it. The end of everything that was, is, and would ever be. Without his Fallen Ring, and with his body beaten and fatigued, there was nothing he could do to stop Eradax. He coughed weakly, resigned to his fate and the extinction of everything he had ever known. Laying his battered head back on the ground, a flicker of movement caught his attention, a subtle movement from under the rubble of a destroyed structure. It was the boy, Simon. He had presumed him dead, but somehow, some way, the young man had seemingly clung to his life.

Viktor chuckled gently. Simon's strength, spirit and courage were admirable. Maybe all was not lost. A technique he had learned during his travels across Asia many years ago flitted across his battle-weary mind. Maybe he could transfer the latent energy left over from his Ring. Perhaps where he had failed against Eradax, Simon might succeed?

Viktor inhaled deeply, raised his hand and shakily traced a triangle from his forehead to his chest. Summoning all of his chi and the green energy that was left within him, he pointed two fingers towards Simon and directed the residual power towards him before losing consciousness, his head lolling on the ground.

***

The Guardian crawled himself up to his hands, his muscles trembling, protesting at every inch of movement. His breath came in ragged gasps and his vision blurred. Trapped beneath the wreckage of the crumbled building, he glanced across the shadowy abyss. His heart began to race. Eradax was activating a large, ominous machine while clutching Viktor's Fallen Ring. He looked across to Viktor's lifeless body on the ground. Vibrant hues of green energy were flowing towards him. What was happening? As the green rays of light reached him, they surrounded him, then flowed into the silver Ring on his finger, lighting up his hand in a dazzling array of purple and green. His skin tingled as a new power coursed through his body, as though he was being charged. Of course, the green energy had come from Viktor. He must have transferred the last vestiges of his strength to him.

The Guardian looked back towards Viktor, who lay bloodied on the ashen ground in the distance. With tenacity burning in his eyes, he turned his attention back to Eradax. The devastation caused by the alien, the harm inflicted on Layla and the catastrophic plan he was about to execute fuelled his fury. All his pain and fears culminated in one driving force, lending him additional valour. His entire being trembled with rage, the voice of the Ring a bolstering force, urging him to stand back up and fight. *No, we didn't come this far only to see your life end like this. This is not how the story ends.*

Summoning his newfound strength, the purple humanoid rose from the dusty ground, his muscles tensed with an unyielding determination. *The mission is not over yet. You know what you must do. For this is our finest hour!* The voice of the Ring fuelled his willpower, encouraging him to overcome the odds. With every atom of strength in his being, he threw off the mountainous tons of debris and stood upright, his steely glare fixed upon Eradax. He was in Omega mode now. Short spikes and armoured plates sprouted from his purple form, and a primal howl of pure outrage escaped his lips, the sheer force of it reverberating through the desolate landscape and drawing Eradax's attention away from his cataclysmic plans.

The shockwaves of the Guardian's anger-fuelled cry amplified the impact of his charge, catching Eradax off guard and slamming him with unrelenting force away from the machine, his grip on Viktor's Ring faltering. The machine trembled in response to the collision, its titanic operation momentarily disrupted.

Eradax struggled to regain his footing, his fiery yellow eyes locked onto the purple humanoid, his face strained with surprise and frustration. 'Impossible! You should be dead!' he yelled.

'No ... I'm not out yet. And I'm mad enough to finish you!' roared the Guardian in response.

Eradax threw up his arms and unleashed a blast of sinister energy towards his rival, but bolstered by the extra green power coursing through his veins, the Guardian withstood the assault. He gritted his teeth and ploughed through the searing energy blast, his unyielding will defusing the attack into nothing more than a minor annoyance.

With every step, the Guardian unloaded an explosive blast of luminous purple and green energy, cracking the ground on which he stood. The broiling aura surrounding him intensified as he barrelled forward, his momentum unwavering. Eradax swung a massive arm towards the Guardian in an attempt to counter his advance, but the Guardian sidestepped the swing, his purple arms transforming into curved blades to deflect the attack. Countering with a powerful strike of his own, he swung his blades, impaling Eradax's arms.

Eradax grunted in pain, his iron-clad skin cracking under the pressure of the Guardian's assault. Ignoring the searing agony that surged through his limbs, Eradax blasted his opponent again, but the Guardian's resoluteness held fast as he weathered the attack.

In a swift and calculated movement, the Guardian disengaged from Eradax's arms, twisting his body to avoid a retaliatory strike. Taking advantage of the opening, the Guardian lunged forward, his blades finding their target once more, this time piercing through Eradax's torso. As Eradax's fiery eyes widened in shock and torment, the purple Guardian's voice rang out with a stern proclamation:

'Your reign of terror ends here. It's time I show you just how powerful I really am!'

With a final surge of strength, the Guardian wrenched his blades upwards, tearing through Eradax's body and wrenching off his head. Grotesque and decapitated, the alien staggered forwards before collapsing onto the dusty soil, the shattered fragments of his metallic skin scattering into the air in a shower of sparks.

The purple Guardian stood over Eradax's corpse, his chest heaving with exhaustion and triumph. The once mighty being had been reduced to a broken heap of debris, his reign of destruction forever silenced. Or at least it appeared that way. The remnants of his fallen enemy lay at his feet, but he couldn't shake the feeling that somewhere, somehow, far across the universe, Eradax's presence lingered on. Whether it was due to the surge of adrenaline or something else, he didn't know, but the feeling was unsettling.

With a deep breath, the Guardian let out a mighty roar, releasing the tension that had gripped him. The battle had been won. But the sense of victory only lasted a few moments before the bombilating sounds of the machine cut through his thoughts.

He turned away from Eradax's crumbling form and looked towards the machine, his heart racing with urgency. There was no time to lose. Swiftly, he began to make his way towards the colossal device, his limping steps echoing through the barren landscape. The machine was a monolithic construct, its intricate mechanisms emanating an eerie and foreboding energy. The air around it crackled with tension, and he could feel the raw power coursing through its core. His eyes narrowed, his mind bubbling away, desperate to comprehend the consequences of its activation.

As he neared the machine, a deafening hum filled his ears, drowning out all other sounds. He stared at the machine's intricate panels and circuitry, the pulsating energy within it growing more intense by the second. He must act now. He had to prevent whatever catastrophic event the machine might unleash upon this realm and beyond. The whirring grew louder, its atomic energy frighteningly unstable. He glanced around and gasped. The fabric of reality surrounding him was beginning to tear open, the walls of existence warping, as if to fold in on itself.

Turning back to the machine, he stared at the complex apparatus, uncertain of how to proceed. In desperation, he appealed to the silver Ring on his finger, his thoughts racing as he sought its guidance and wisdom. The Ring hesitated, its violet glow flickering slightly before it responded to his silent plea. *To stop the operation of the Infinity Forge, a sacrifice must be made*. The tone was grave and solemn.

Simon's heart sank at the weight of the revelation. The words hung heavily in the air, their implications echoing through his mind. *A sacrifice?* The price for stopping the machine was something he must give up? But the Ring's answer left him grappling with uncertainty. What would the sacrifice entail? And, more importantly, what would he be required to sacrifice?

The air around him grew colder, the sense of dread intensifying as the machine's energy surged, casting an eerie glow across the shadowy landscape. The fate of this realm and the cosmos itself was hanging in the balance, and the weight of responsibility was continuing to press down on him.

Fighting his fear, he took a step closer to the machine, his fingers brushing against the intricate symbols etched on its surface. As he contemplated the choices before him, the words of the Ring echoed in his ears: *One must stand and make the ultimate sacrifice for the cosmos. If you survive this, nothing will ever be the same. The reality and everything you know will be changed indefinitely.*

The turbulent energy beam continued to surge into the sky, its light slicing through the bleak surroundings. What sacrifice must he make? And would it be enough to save the universe from impending catastrophe?

CHAPTER 20

Viktor's knees sank into the grimy ground of the Shadow Plane, his eyes fixed on the towering beam of chaotic energy that pierced the bleak sky. Nearby, next to the colossal machine, stood the young man, reverting to his human form with panic etched across his features. The alien enemy may have been overthrown, but clearly the chaos was far from over. They were still in a dire situation. Observing the young man, Viktor recalled his past desires for power and domination. Years of being trapped within the desolate expanse of the Shadow Plane had chipped away at those ambitions, replacing them with a begrudging acceptance of the world's current state. Eradax's madness, if left unchecked, could unravel the very fabric of reality, leaving nothing in its wake.

Pushing himself up from the ash-covered ground, Vicktor spat the blood from his mouth and gritted his teeth, his torn clothes fluttering as he staggered towards the machine. He glanced at Simon and saw fear and uncertainty in the young man's eyes. It was a similar fear that had once driven him, which had led him down a path of violent conquest.

Reaching the machine, Viktor examined it briefly. Eradax's twisted dream was perilously close to realisation. He turned to Simon, determination in his voice. 'What can we do?'

Simon's frantic gaze shifted between Viktor and the machine. 'The Ring told me ... that a sacrifice is needed to stop it. That one must stand and make the ultimate sacrifice for the cosmos. One must bear that brunt.'

Viktor's heart pounded, his thoughts racing. A sacrifice – a bitter irony that seemed to follow him from his past. He let out a sigh, a sad smile tugging at his lips. The irony was not lost on him: a man who had once sought dominion over the world, now standing here ready to give everything to save it all. Make no mistake, though, the world still needed direction, but perhaps in his absence, the young man, once his rival, could provide that direction, albeit in a different direction.

'Listen, Simon.' Viktor's voice was hoarse, but firm. 'There's only one way to stop this. You need to get out of here. Open a portal and leave.'

Simon's eyes widened, his voice shaking. 'I can't just leave you here, Viktor. Not this time. We'll find another way.'

Viktor's expression hardened as he took a step closer to Simon, his voice firm. 'You must. If this machine isn't stopped, Eradax's madness will consume everything. I've already seen much destruction, so I can't let that happen.'

A turbulent mix of emotions flooded Simon's eyes: fear, determination and a trace of admiration. He clenched his fists, as if struggling with an internal battle. 'I won't abandon you like this. There has to be another way.'

Viktor's tone softened, his eyes locking with Simon's. 'Simon, you've already shown me that there's still honour left in this ambiguous world. You have the chance to uphold that. And the people you care about need you. So, leave this place, and remember that you are the world's protector. Besides, it's my Ring that's in there, not yours.'

As Simon hesitated, Viktor slipped his finger into his obsidian Ring. He focused on the machine, a solemn understanding settling in. The hum of energy was building within it, ready to unleash untold destruction upon the cosmos. This was his only choice – the final act that could redeem his tumultuous past.

With that, Viktor shouted, his voice punctuated with pain and resolve. 'Open a portal, Simon. Do it! Do it now!'

Simon's shoulders slumped, anger and helplessness clouding his eyes. He looked at Viktor, his voice cracking with emotion. 'Goodbye, Viktor.'

As Simon created a shimmering portal, Viktor's grip tightened around his Ring. With one last glance at the young man who had unknowingly helped him find redemption, he thrust his obsidian Ring into the heart of the machine. The moment the Ring connected, a blinding flash of energy surged from the machine, enveloping Viktor whose screams filled the air, merging with the machine's thunderous rumble as the full force of the cosmos consumed him.

***

Simon watched in horror as the energy of the cosmos swirled around Viktor, an otherworldly storm of power and dazzling light. The beam of energy wavered, then began to flicker and fade. As the blinding light subsided, the machine imploded with a deafening roar, leaving behind only ashes and echoes of Viktor's last stand.

Opening another portal, Simon leaped through it before it zipped shut after him, allowing him to escape the deadly doomsday that had laid waste to the Shadow Plane.

CHAPTER 21

Simon stepped through the swirling portal, his heart heavy with relief and sorrow. The ordinariness of the alleyway he was standing in was in stark contrast to the nightmarish realm he had left behind. The Shadow Plane's eerie landscape and the cataclysmic events were still fresh in his mind, a jumble of emotions swirling within him. Even though he had escaped the cataclysmic event, the rumble of its aftermath had followed him to this world, the ground subtly quaking beneath his feet.

He took a deep breath and exhaled loudly, relief flooding his body. The air tasted different, cleaner than the tainted atmosphere of the desolate plane in that otherworldly dimension. His senses had been assaulted by the turmoil of the battle and now the normalcy of his surroundings felt almost surreal. He leaned against the cold brick wall, closing his eyes for a moment to steady himself. Viktor's sacrifice resonated deeply with him. His brave act stirred a mixture of gratitude and sadness in Simon's heart. He had lost an enemy, a rival, but he had also lost a complicated ally who had put aside his own well-being to save countless others. He could not help but admire Viktor's selflessness, despite his dubious past actions.

Pushing away from the wall, Simon shook his head as if to clear his thoughts. He couldn't afford to linger in the past; there was much to do in the present. His thoughts shifted to Layla, his worries for her resurfacing. The events in the Shadow Plane had momentarily pushed her out of his mind, but now concern came flooding back. He must go to her.

With determined but painful strides, he began to make his way to the hospital. Layla could never imagine in her wildest dreams what he had just gone through. But he couldn't wait to share the story with her, nonetheless.

Chapter 22

Layla's eyes fluttered open, the sterile fluorescent light of the hospital room washing over her. She blinked a few times, trying to clear the haze that clouded her memory, wincing at the dull throbbing in her head. Slowly the pieces began to slot together as she recalled the events that had led her to this hospital bed.

There had been an attack. A sudden rush of panic gripped her heart as she remembered the alien figure and the explosion that had knocked her off her feet. She struggled to sit up, her head spinning from the effort. As she glanced around the room disorientated, her heart leaped with joy and relief at the sight of Simon standing in the doorway.

'Simon,' she whispered, her voice hoarse.

He rushed to her side, his expression a mix of relief and concern. As he took her hand in his, a comforting warmth flooded through her.

'Layla,' he murmured, his voice a soothing balm to her anxious mind. 'It's a blessing to see you awake.'

Layla smiled weakly. 'What happened? I remember … something attacked us. You transformed and then everything went dark.'

Simon's gaze softened as he looked into her eyes. 'Yeah, Layla. We … were attacked by an evil alien. But we're safe now.'

Layla's brow furrowed. 'Did you … did you defeat it?'

Simon hesitated for a moment before answering. 'Yeah, and I had help too. Help … from an unexpected place.'

Layla sighed in relief, the weight of the fear and worry lifting away. She reached up and touched the side of her head, wincing at the tenderness. 'I can't remember everything clearly.'

Simon's grip on her hand tightened gently. 'It's okay. You took a hit, but you're going to be all right. You just need to rest and recover.'

Layla nodded softly, her eyes never leaving Simon's face. A mix of emotions swirled within her – gratitude for his presence, worry about what they had faced and something else, something deeper that she couldn't quite name.

'You gave me quite a scare, you know,' Simon said, concern evident in his eyes.

Layla smiled, the warmth of his touch spreading through her like a comforting embrace. 'Sorry about that.'

'I'm just glad you're okay,' he said softly.

As they sat together in the quiet of the hospital room, Layla's mind began to drift. There were still a lot of mysteries surrounding Simon: the transformation, his powers and the silver Ring he wore. But more importantly, he had shown such strength and determination in the face of danger.

'Simon,' she began, her voice hesitant. 'There's something I want to say.'

He looked at her, his eyes curious and attentive. 'What is it, Layla?'

She took a deep breath, her heart pounding in her chest. 'I want you to know that I'm here for you, no matter what. Whatever you're going through, whatever secrets you have ... I want you to trust me and share them with me.'

Simon looked deeply into her eyes, and she could see a mixture of emotions: gratitude, empathy and something else, something vulnerable that made her heart ache.

'Layla,' he said, his voice soft but steady. 'You have no idea how much those words mean to me.'

She gave his hand a reassuring squeeze. 'I'm in this with you, Simon. Whatever challenges come your way, I want to face them with you.'

He smiled, a genuine, heartfelt smile. 'Thank you, Layla. I promise I'll tell you everything.'

As they sat there, hand in hand, Layla felt a sense of intense hope. The road ahead might be uncertain, filled with challenges and mysteries, but they would navigate it together. Because she knew that their bond was stronger than any darkness they might face.

CHAPTER 23

Simon's eyes fluttered in the dim light of the hospital room. Layla, his beloved twin flame was lying on the bed, the soft rise and fall of her breath a comfort. Their earlier conversation and her smile had been a balm for his weary soul. Now she was sleeping, her face serene, untouched by the turmoil that had recently shaken their world. He sighed gently, a deep and much-needed sense of peace flowing through him.

As he watched over her, the minutes grew into hours and weariness began to creep up on him. His exhaustion from the earlier battle took over as the last remnants of adrenaline drained from him. His body yearned for rest. With his eyelids growing heavier by the second, he surrendered to the siren call of sleep in the armchair by Layla's bed.

Transitioning into the realm of dreams, he was whisked away into another dimension, a place that felt both surreal and vividly real. He was standing on top of a mighty mountain, with verdant hills and azure skies stretching in all directions. The beauty held him spellbound. This was no earthly vista. With such perfection, it couldn't be, could it?

He glanced at his hand instinctively, but the silver Ring was conspicuously absent. This realisation anchored him. This was not the world he knew. It was a world beyond his imagination. In a slow and deliberate arc, he turned to survey his surroundings.

Behind him, grandeur beyond mortal architecture awaited. Pillars that stretched so high they seemed to touch the very heavens formed the façade of an ancient temple, a testament to craftsmanship that surpassed human hands. Intrigued by such an Olympian sight, he took a step forwards. It was as if he was being beckoned towards the magnificent structure.

As he crossed the threshold, awe coursed through him. The grandeur of the gold, silver, platinum and other precious metals that decorated the grand chamber was unrivalled. His footsteps echoing through the hallway, he looked up at the shimmering walls which were adorned with intricate murals depicting what seemed to be the history of the cosmos. It was truly a sight to behold.

At the end of the hallway, he arrived at a room of such splendour that it seemed to defy comprehension. And it was then that he saw a familiar face – that of the old Superlunary, Cornelius.

His regal robes swirled around him as he turned to face Simon, a smile illuminating his features. Simon's heart soared at the sight of his old friend and mentor. Cornelius's immaculate, dark, silky hair was still slicked back and he barely looked a day older. The projected avatar was just as Simon remembered it. Without a second thought, he rushed over, eager to greet his old mentor.

'Ah, there he is, the protector of not only London but of the whole universe,' said Cornelius as he greeted Simon.

As they spoke, their words echoed in the hallowed halls, bridging the gap between mortal and cosmic. In that ethereal space, Cornelius's presence was both grounding and transcendent, the embodiment of power tempered by vast wisdom.

'Why am I here?' Simon asked, although he suspected he already knew the answer.

Cornelius looked upon the young man with fondness and a pride that seemed to traverse aeons. 'You stand here before me, Simon, because in the heat of your battles you have demonstrated most admirable qualities. Strength, honour, integrity, they course through you like the blood through your veins. You've shielded lives, safeguarded worlds and consistently reflected on your choices. Most recently, you faced Eradax, the renegade who was a threat to reality itself. But in the face of it all, you stood tall and in doing so inspired others. That is noble indeed.'

Simon's chest swelled with a mix of humility and pride. To hear such words from Cornelius, to know his deeds had meaning beyond the immediate, stirred something profound within him.

'Your efforts have not gone unnoticed, Simon. As a result, you have earned an extraordinary commendation. One that goes beyond anything you could possibly fathom,' Cornelius said, holding his hand out to the young man. 'In extending my hand to you, I am offering you a place among us, the Superlunary Ones. If you accept, you will ascend and stand beside us, and one step removed from the Cosmic Being. The One Above All. Unparalleled knowledge, wisdom and immortality will be bestowed upon you. You will transcend your mortal frame and become a primordial. What say you, Simon Jones? Will you join us?'

The weight of the decision hung heavy in the air, a decision that spanned realms and eternity. It was not one to be taken lightly. With such an ascension, he would become a true titan of time, an observer of worlds and keeper of the order of the universe. He would exist and operate in a higher dimension. But what about those he held dear? He couldn't forget them – his beloved Layla, and the life he still wished to lead on Earth. He couldn't leave them, not when there were still more chapters to write.

Simon sighed heavily. 'May I postpone my decision ... to later?'

Cornelius's eyes gleamed with understanding and amusement. 'Yes, Simon, you may do so. But know this. Should you decline our offer now, you will have to pass from the Earth as a mortal first. To die and then be reborn into this dimension.'

Simon nodded. 'Thank you, Cornelius.'

Cornelius smiled, his eyes twinkling with promise. 'We shall meet again, Simon. Not in your dreams but in your reality. And when that day comes, you shall have an audience not just with me but also with your friend James and with the Cosmic Being.'

'I look forward to that,' Simon said, tears streaming down his face. To have been honoured in such a way was deeply emotional and liberating. He breathed a sigh of relief. It was good to know of the rewards that awaited him.

'This great honour is a testament to your character, your will and your ambition. Continue on, Simon. Continue on and fulfil your destiny,' Cornelius said, placing a gentle hand on his shoulder.

With that, the dream began to wane, the vivid colours dimming. Simon's surroundings shifted and like sand running through fingers, the dream slipped away and he awoke in the hospital room. Layla was still asleep in the bed next to his chair. He glanced at the clock near the door. Only a few minutes had passed since he'd drifted off. Yet he could have sworn that the dream had lasted much longer.

Simon rubbed his eyes and yawned. In that brief, profound slumber, he had glimpsed a world full of possibility beyond the bounds of space and time. But a choice lay ahead of him – and one that would shape far more than his own destiny.

CHAPTER 24

Simon walked hand in hand with Layla, the warm glow of the sun gently embracing the bustling streets of London. It was a beautiful day, a day of renewal and reconnection. Layla's recovery had been progressing well, and Simon felt a burst of happiness wash over him as he looked at her smiling face.

'So, you're saying you literally stopped a mad alien's twisted plot and saved the world?' Layla asked, her eyes wide with admiration.

Simon chuckled, his cheeks reddening. 'Well, when you put it that way, it sounds quite grandiose. But yeah, that's the gist of it.'

Layla shook her head in amazement. 'I can't believe you've been keeping all this from me.'

Simon shrugged. 'Well, it wasn't something I could just casually bring up during dinner conversations.'

They both laughed, the sound of their joy blending harmoniously with the rhythm of the city. Simon had felt the weight lift from his shoulders as he shared more of his secrets with Layla. It was liberating to let someone in, to know that he didn't have to carry the burden alone anymore.

As they walked on, he recounted the events that had unfolded in the Shadow Plane: the battle against Eradax and the sacrifice of Viktor Nemesis. Layla listened attentively, her eyes reflecting a mix of emotions – awe, concern and pride.

'You faced all that with just the Ring?' Layla asked, her voice tinged with worry.

Simon nodded, his gaze fixed on the path ahead. 'Yes, though I had Viktor's help, especially when I needed it most.'

Layla squeezed his hand. 'You're truly something else, Simon. So much braver than I ever could have thought. You're ... you're phenomenal. I can't believe I'm dating a real-life superhero.'

Touched by her words, Simon chuckled again. 'I don't know about superhero, but I did what I had to.'

They walked in comfortable silence for a while, content in each other's presence. Simon stole glances at Layla, amazed by the resilience she had shown after the initial incident.

'I'm just glad you're safe,' Layla said softly, breaking the silence.

Simon smiled broadly. 'I'm glad you're safe too, Layla. That's all that mattered to me.'

As they walked past an electrical shop, Layla's gaze was drawn to a TV screen in the shop window. The news was on and they were showing clips of the alien attack that had taken place at the docks a couple of weeks earlier. Simon followed her gaze and sighed, the memories of that day still vivid in his mind.

'Simon,' Layla began, turning to him, 'are you going to keep doing your vigilante thing as the Elusive Guardian?'

Simon paused for a moment. The truth was, the events in the Shadow Plane had made him re-evaluate his priorities. He had come face to face with the cosmic consequences of his life as the Guardian – he had even come close to death – and all of it had given him a newfound perspective.

He looked deeply into Layla's eyes, his expression sincere. 'I'm putting it on the back burner for now. I want to focus on the things that truly matter, like you and my family.'

Layla smiled, her eyes shimmering with happiness. 'I'd like that.'

'Besides,' Simon continued, his tone teasing, 'I think I've had my fill of epic battles for a while.'

Layla laughed and glanced at him playfully. 'So, am I the only one who gets to know your secret identity?'

Simon chuckled. 'For now, yes. I'm not ready for the whole world to know just yet.'

Layla nudged him with her elbow. 'I feel like I'm part of an exclusive club now.'

Simon grinned. 'Well, you should.' With those words, he leaned in, capturing the moment with a gentle kiss. He could sense Layla's happiness in the way she responded, the warmth of her smile against his lips, a silent affirmation of the special bond they shared.

And as they pulled away, a mutual smile lingered, leaving them both feeling a bit giddy.

As they headed home, chatting and laughing, Simon sighed deeply with contentment. Filled with a warmth he had never known before, he looked at Layla. The day would soon arrive when he would choose an elegant ring with which to propose to her.

A familiar voice interrupted his thoughts: *How about a Fallen Ring?*

Simon could only chuckle. *Sounds like you need to work on your humour*! If the silver Ring had a face, he thought, it would probably be smiling.

The sun began to set, casting a golden hue over the city. Simon and Layla walked off into the early evening, their steps in sync and their hearts connected as they ventured towards an uncharted, yet optimistic and exciting future.

Epilogue

In the Northern Hemisphere, below the celestial display of auroras that graced the night skies with their enchanting dances, stood the ancient and powerful Superlunary Cornelius. Wrapped in a thick brown overcoat that swayed gently in the cold breeze, he gazed up at the mesmerising lights that swirled in the heavens. Beside him stood a young Superlunary, one who had not long been formed from the ether light.

Cornelius turned to his companion, his voice bearing the weight of a wisdom that transcended time. 'You see, my friend,' he began, 'not everything is as it seems. There are nuances in the universe and in those that inhabit it. Take the beings from Earth, for instance. They form a vast array of differing types. The more you observe them, the more you see.'

The young Superlunary regarded the auroras thoughtfully before responding, their tone carrying a sense of scepticism.

'Perhaps. But aren't humans selfish, petty and quarrelsome? They're often drawn to their innermost desires, causing much chaos and suffering.'

Cornelius nodded. 'Yes, you are right. Humans are capable of many vile actions. But amid the darkness, there are moments that shine with brilliance, moments that remind us of their potential for greatness.'

His companion's gaze remained fixed on the auroras as they danced across the sky. 'You truly believe that?' they asked, their voice tinged with doubt.

Cornelius smiled gently, his eyes reflecting the aeons of knowledge he carried. 'Indeed. Allow me to share a tale, one that showcases the remarkable capacity of a single human, one who defied the odds.'

The young Superlunary turned to look at Cornelius with a quizzical look.

'His name is Simon Jones,' Cornelius began, his voice captivating and compelling. 'A young man who stumbled upon a Fallen Ring, an instrument of immense power. Rather than continuing to succumb to its allure, he chose to wield its power responsibly.'

As the auroras continued their celestial ballet above, Cornelius recounted Simon's journey. He spoke of the battles the young man had fought and the nights spent as the vigilante defender of his city. He detailed Simon's valiant encounter with Eradax, the formidable force that threatened to plunge the universe into oblivion.

His companion listened intently, drawn into the narrative of such a unique human being, their eyes growing wider as Cornelius shared the complexities of Simon's choices, his struggles and the sacrifices he had made.

With a hint of pride in his voice, Cornelius spoke of Simon's unwavering courage. 'He rose above his temptations and the challenges that faced him, ultimately playing a pivotal role in saving the world and universe itself from utter destruction. His actions influenced the very outcome that cradles the cosmos.'

The young Superlunary nodded in acknowledgement, their scepticism giving way to a growing sense of admiration. 'To think that a single human could hold such power and wield it responsibly, and at such a tender age, is remarkable,' they mused.

Cornelius looked away into the distance, his voice carrying both fondness and hope. 'Simon's journey reminds us that even in the face of immense challenges, there are individuals who will rise above their circumstances to create change. It also reminds us that we must consider deeply every decision we make. Simon's tale has been etched into the cosmos, along with others who have had a positive impact on the world. This young man's story will be told for generations to come.'

The ethereal light of the dancing auroras created an almost spiritual light across the night sky as Cornelius continued to express his admiration for Simon's spirit. He wished him well, his words resonating with the hope that humanity, despite its flaws, would strive for something greater.

The young Superlunary absorbed Cornelius's words, the silence between them allowing the weight of those insights to settle. The stars above shimmered as if in agreement, aligning with the wisdom shared.

With a final nod, Cornelius concluded his thoughts, the depth of his insight lingering in the air. As they stood beneath the cosmic spectacle, the two Superlunary beings shared a moment of quiet reflection, contemplating the potential of humanity amid the vast tapestry of existence as the auroras shimmered across the night sky, casting a radiant glow over the ever-unfolding story of creation.

Acknowledgements

Books are not one-person endeavours. Creating them and getting them out to readers is a commitment that takes dedication. That's why I am so grateful to my editor, my aunt and to all of you who supported and helped make this book possible. I could not have done it without you!

About the Author

Key Dawkins is a writer and author from the UK. Since childhood, he's always wanted to write and publish a book. This is his third one within the young adult and thriller genre, following the first and second *The Fallen Ring* novellas.

Milton Keynes UK
Ingram Content Group UK Ltd.
UKHW011911120724
445574UK00004B/188

9 781739 618643